Tales from Africa

OTHER OXFORD COLLECTIONS

Tales from
Africa

Retold by Kathleen Arnott

Illustrated by Rosamund Fowler

OXFORD
UNIVERSITY PRESS

To Margaret and Rosemary
With Love

OXFORD
UNIVERSITY PRESS

Great Clarendon Street, Oxford OX2 6DP

Oxford University Press is a department of the University of Oxford.
It furthers the University's objective of excellence in research, scholarship,
and education by publishing worldwide in

Oxford New York
Athens Auckland Bangkok Bogotá Buenos Aires Calcutta
Cape Town Chennai Dar es Salaam Delhi Florence Hong Kong Istanbul
Karachi Kuala Lumpur Madrid Melbourne Mexico City Mumbai
Nairobi Paris São Paulo Singapore Taipei Tokyo Toronto Warsaw

and associated companies in Berlin Ibadan

Oxford is a registered trade mark of Oxford University Press
in the UK and in certain other countries

British Library Cataloguing in Publication Data available

ISBN 0 19 275079 8

Typeset by AFS Image Setters Ltd, Glasgow

Printed in Great Britain
by Cox & Wyman Ltd, Reading, Berkshire

Contents

I am indebted to my husband, Dr David W. Arnott,
for the translation into English of several of his
recordings of Hausa and Fulani stories, and also for his
considerable help in the selection of the rest of
the material.

Why the Dog is the Friend of Man

Long, long ago the jackal and the dog were brothers and lived together in the wild bush. Each day they would go hunting together, and when evening fell they would return to the valley which was their only home, and share their food.

One night they both came back empty-handed and ravenously hungry, and to make matters worse, a cold wind was blowing across the bush and the animals could not find any protection from the gale.

'Alas!' said the dog. 'It is a very bad thing to feel hungry, but much worse to feel both hungry and cold at the same time.'

'Lie down and go to sleep,' suggested the jackal. 'Then when the morning comes we can go hunting again and perhaps catch that young deer we so nearly caught today.'

But the dog could not sleep. His stomach rumbled and his teeth chattered, for his hairy coat was less warm than the jackal's. As he lay on the ground, his eyes wide open in misery, he caught sight of a red glow in the distance.

'Jackal!' he exclaimed. 'What is that light over there?'

'That's a village, and the red is a man's fire,' explained the jackal.

'Fire is warm,' said the dog longingly. 'Won't you go and fetch me some fire, Jackal? You are braver than I.'

'Certainly not!' growled the jackal. 'You fetch it yourself if you want it. It was your idea.'

But the dog was afraid of Man and he curled up even smaller on the bare ground to try to keep himself warm. As he lay there, he thought that perhaps the people in the village were eating and he wondered whether they might leave some bones lying on the ground after their meal, which he could creep in and steal. The thought made him hungrier and hungrier, so that presently he forgot his fear and said boldly to the jackal:

'I can't stay here in the cold any longer. I am going to the village and will try to get some fire. Perhaps I may even bring back some bones for you too. If I don't get back soon, call me, in case I cannot find my way to you.'

So off ran the dog towards the red glow in the village, and when he was nearly there he slowed down and crept in on his stomach, hoping that no one would hear him. Nearer and nearer he got to the fire, sniffing eagerly as he smelt the odour of a past meal still lingering in the air. Just as he reached the dying embers of the fire outside the door of a hut, some fowls roosting in a nearby tree gave the alarm. A man rushed out and caught him, lifting high his spear and saying:

'What are you doing in my compound, you thieving dog?'

'Oh, please don't kill me,' begged the dog. 'I have not

come to harm anybody here, but only to get a little warmth from your dying fire. I beg you, let me lie down here to rest and to warm myself, and later I will go back to the bush and never trouble you again.'

The dog looked so cold and miserable that the man, who was kind at heart, felt sorry for him. He put down his spear and said:

'Very well. If you promise not to harm anyone in this village you may lie down by the fire. But when you are warm, you must go back to the bush again.'

The dog thanked him profusely and lay down beside the fire, on which the man piled some more sticks and blew them into a blaze. Now the dog was happy indeed, for under his very nose lay a bone which someone had thrown down at the end of their meal. He gnawed away happily for some time, while the heat from the fire warmed his shivering limbs. Never had he been so contented or so comfortable.

Suddenly the man called from inside his hut:

'Aren't you warm yet?'

'Not quite,' answered the dog, who had just seen another bone nearby that he wanted to chew.

'Well, I'll give you a little longer,' said the man, and all was quiet again except for the cracking of bones under the dog's strong teeth.

'Aren't you warm yet?' asked the man presently.

But the dog thought unhappily of the cold wind blowing across the bush, and creeping even closer to the fire he begged:

'Let me stay just a little longer.'

It was some time before the man called out again, for both he and the dog at his door had been fast asleep.

'You must have finished warming yourself by now,'

said the man, rising to his feet and coming out of his hut.

The dog, deciding that honesty was the best policy, looked into the man's eyes and said:

'Yes, I am warm now, but I do not want to go back to the bush, where I am so often cold and hungry. Will you not let me stay in the village with you? I will help you hunt the birds that fly in the forest. I will teach you the cunning ways of the wild animals so that you can kill them for food, and I promise you that unlike my brother the jackal, I will never rob you of your goats and chickens. All I ask in return is a place by your fire and the remains of your meal.'

The man now looked closely into the dog's eyes and saw that he was speaking the truth.

'Very well,' he replied. 'If you promise to serve and obey me I will give you warmth and food.'

Ever since that day, the dog has lived with man. But when at night you hear the jackal calling 'Bo-aa! Bo-aa!' from the bush, you will know that he is calling for his brother the dog, to return to him with the fire and the bones that he went to fetch. But the dog never answers the call and the jackal wanders the bush alone.

The Man who Learned the
Language of the Animals

Ohia was a very unlucky man. Everything he did went wrong. If he sowed corn, the seed would be eaten up by birds or carried off by ants. If he planted cassava, monkeys would come and dig it up. If he bought a goat, it would soon die, and if he tried to keep hens, they would lay their eggs in the forest where he could not find them.

Now Ohia had a wife called Ariwehu, but as she was equally unlucky in all she undertook they were soon so poor that they scarcely had anything left to eat, and only one threadbare cloth each to wear.

One evening when they had eaten a very meagre supper, they sat outside their hut and discussed the future.

'Surely there is something we can do to get money,' said Ariwehu mournfully. 'If I do not buy a new cloth soon this one will fall to pieces and then I shall be ashamed to go into the village and will have to stay all day in our hut.'

Ohia sat dejectedly on a big log, holding his head with his hands.

'Yes, we must think of something,' he replied. 'I never remember feeling so hungry as I do tonight, and that was the last of our yams we've just eaten, so there will be nothing at all to eat tomorrow unless our friends take pity on us.'

He thought hard and his wife sighed deeply, while the owls in the forest behind the village hooted mournfully in the dark night.

At last Ohia had an idea.

'I know what I can do,' he suddenly exclaimed, looking almost cheerful again. 'I will go to that rich farmer who lives on the other side of the hill and ask him if I may cut down some of his palm trees for him. He has so many that I'm sure he will agree. Then I will collect the sap from the trees for palm wine and you, my wife, can take the wine to market and sell it.'

'I would willingly do that,' said the wife, and she closed her eyes imagining how she would spend the money, and deciding on the colour of the new cloth she would buy.

The next day Ohia rose very early and went to call on the rich farmer. He proved to be a very reasonable man and even lent Ohia some earthenware pots in which to collect the sap, only making him promise to divide any money he earned between the two of them, since they were not Ohia's trees.

Ohia was delighted and set to work with a will, cutting down seven big palm trees. It was hard labour, especially for a man with an empty stomach, but at last it was finished and he was able to make a cut in each tree underneath which he put a pot in which to collect the sap.

That night Ohia and his wife lay awake several hours, discussing what they would do when they had sold the palm wine and had money in their hands at last, and long before daybreak Ohia went with a lighted torch to see how much palm wine he had collected in his pots. He hoped to bring it home for his wife to take to market that very day.

When he reached the first tree he was disappointed to find that something had knocked over the pot and broken it to fragments, spilling all the sap. But he did not think much about it as he knew he had six more trees waiting for him further on.

Alas! The second pot had been broken too, and the third and the fourth, and before he reached the seventh pot he had already guessed that they would all be shattered to pieces, as indeed they were.

He hurried back to his wife, almost in tears at the misfortune that had befallen them.

'Alas!' he cried, 'I knew it would be no good. Everything I attempt is doomed to fail, I may as well lie down and die.'

'Nonsense,' said his wife briskly. 'You must not give in. I expect it was a thief who stole the wine and then broke the pots to make it look as though some wild animal had kicked them over.'

'Yes, you are probably right,' replied her husband. 'I will try again.'

So he borrowed some more pots from his friends, for he had no money with which to buy any in the market, and placed them carefully beneath each tree so that the sap from the cut he had made would run into each pot.

But the next morning he was in despair again when he discovered that the same thing had happened and all the pots were broken. He was certain that it was the work of a thief, so he said to his wife:

'Tonight I will set some more pots in place, but I will not be such a fool as to leave them unguarded. I will hide nearby and watch for the thief and when I have caught him I will make him pay for his wickedness.'

Somehow Ohia and his wife managed to borrow a few more pots from their long-suffering friends, and when he had put them in the right position to catch the sap, he hid behind a large tree-trunk and waited.

For a long time nothing happened and Ohia got cramped and cold as he sat silent and motionless, not even daring to slap at the mosquitoes which bit his face, in case he warned the thief. Then, at about two o'clock in the morning, he saw a dark shape moving towards the nearest palm tree and heard the sound of a breaking pot.

Creeping soundlessly up to the figure he was amazed to find a full-grown deer carrying a large pot of its own, into which it emptied Ohia's sap and then broke Ohia's pot.

With a mighty leap, Ohia landed beside the deer and reached out a hand to seize it. But the animal was too quick for him and leaving its own large pot on the ground, it ran swiftly away into the forest. Ohia was determined not to lose sight of it and his anger added speed to his strides, as he chased after the animal for many miles.

At last the sun began to rise but Ohia had not yet caught up with the deer, and it was not until some hours later that they reached the bottom of a steep hill, up which the animal ran with faltering steps. Ohia was almost exhausted too but climbed slowly upwards, until he suddenly discovered himself in the middle of a large assemblage of animals grouped around a regal-looking leopard, who was obviously their king.

The deer lay panting at the king's feet, and told his story, while all the animals turned and fixed their eyes on Ohia, who then begged the leopard to hear his side of the tale.

So beginning with the story of his continuous ill-luck, Ohia explained why he had chased the deer into the leopard's kingdom and begged him to excuse his intrusion into animal-land.

The leopard king listened attentively and said:

'We all agree that it is the deer who was doing wrong, not you, O man. I had given the deer plenty of money to buy palm wine for me, but he decided it would be cheaper to steal yours. We will, therefore, present you with a gift in exchange for the wine the deer has stolen and the pots he has broken. From now onwards you will have the power to understand the speech of all animals, and in time, this will make you a rich man.'

Ohia could not see how such a gift would bring him wealth, but he bowed to the king and thanked him politely.

'One thing you must remember, however,' said the king. 'You must never tell anyone else about your wonderful gift. If you do, you will die at once.'

Ohia thanked him again and promised never to speak about the gift to anyone, and then he slowly climbed down the hill to begin his long journey home.

Ariwehu was delighted to see him and plied him with questions, but all he would tell her was that he had caught a deer breaking his pots, and had chased after it without catching it.

The next evening he had one last attempt to get sap

from the palm trees, for not all the pots had been broken by the deer. How delighted the poor man was to find his jars overflowing with sap, which his wife quickly took to market and sold for a good price.

Now Ohia's fortunes changed indeed. He always found plenty of palm wine to sell, and was able to buy goats and chickens and have his house repaired, while his wife had more clothes than she knew what to do with, and a little son was born to them at last.

One morning while he was bathing in a nearby pool, Ohia heard a chicken talking to her young ones.

'Look at that stupid man in the river,' she clucked. 'How very unpleasant it must be to have water all over one's body. But it's quite obvious he is a fool, because he doesn't even know there are three jars of gold buried behind his house. I uncovered them myself while I was scratching for food, but since I don't like the man, I covered them up again before he saw them.'

Ohia could scarcely believe his ears, but went on washing himself as though he had heard nothing. Later in the day, when the rest of the village was sleeping in the heat of the afternoon, Ohia dug in his garden and soon found the three jars of gold.

There was enough money to keep him in comfort for the rest of his life, but he had to hide it away under the floor of his house, since he could not tell his wife how he had known where to dig.

Now life became very pleasant for Ohia and Ariwehu, for they were the richest couple in the village. Ariwehu was a kind woman and helped any poor people who came to her in trouble, but Ohia wanted to become even more respected and he decided to buy a second wife.

The foolish man chose a woman whose good looks

made him blind to her jealous nature, and as soon as he brought her into his home, trouble began. The new wife could not bear to see Ohia and Ariwehu together, and if they spoke or laughed when she was near, she flew into a rage and accused them of ridiculing her. She crept around the compound, listening to all they said, always ready to complain or to weep if she heard so much as a sentence pass their lips.

Poor Ohia! He tried very hard to keep the peace, but all in vain.

Then one evening, Ohia was sitting outside his house with Ariwehu beside him, neither daring to speak, since the new wife was close at hand. Ariwehu was tired and was gently dozing, when Ohia heard two little mice talking in the roof above his head.

'As soon as these people have gone inside to sleep,' squeaked a mouse, 'we will raid their larder.'

'O yes!' piped the other mouse. 'I've just been looking inside it and they have some lovely bean cakes that I can't wait to get my teeth into.'

Ohia laughed aloud, forgetting there were other people near him. Ariwehu woke with a start, but the new wife rushed out of the next hut, exclaiming:

'There you go again, poking fun at me. What were the two of you laughing at?'

Ariwehu insisted that she had been asleep, and Ohia explained that it was just a foolish thought that had come to him, but the woman would not believe them.

'If you were really laughing at a mere foolish thought, you would tell me at once what it was,' she complained, and for the rest of the evening and all the following day she worried and nagged at him to tell her the joke. Finally, in desperation, she decided to go to the chief and lodge a complaint against her husband. Now the chief was a friend of Ohia's and when he heard the angry tale of the new wife, he sent for Ohia, meaning to help him.

'Surely it would be better to tell this new wife of yours what you were laughing at, than to have all your days and nights made miserable by her moaning,' the chief said to him.

Ohia was in a fix, for he respected the chief and was indeed tired of the way his new wife had spoilt his new-found happiness. For some moments he sat silent, trying to decide on the best course to take, and at last he resigned himself to death, since he knew he would have to tell his long-kept secret.

He called all his friends and relatives to a big feast during which he stood up and announced that he bequeathed all his gold to Ariwehu and all his property to his son. Then he bowed to the chief, bade him goodbye, and told the assembled company the story of his meeting with the leopard king and the gift he had given him. He only had time to tell them why he had laughed that evening on hearing the mice speak, when he fell dead, just as the king had warned him he would.

Then the feast was turned into a funeral, and all his friends wept and mourned as they buried Ohia. So angry were they with his new wife for being the cause of his death, that they seized her and killed her and burnt her body outside the village. Her ashes were scattered by the wind over all the earth, and wherever a speck of her dust fell, jealousy and selfishness took root. And this was the beginning of evil in the world, where only kindness and unselfishness had existed before.

Tortoise and the Lizard

Tortoise had used up all his salt, and he found his meals so tasteless without it that he decided to call on his brother and ask him if he had any to spare. His brother had plenty.

'How will you get it back to your home?' he asked Tortoise.

'If you will wrap the salt in a piece of bark cloth, and tie it up with string, then I can put the string over my shoulder and drag the parcel along the ground behind me,' said Tortoise.

'A splendid idea!' exclaimed his brother, and between them they made a tidy package of the salt. Then Tortoise set off for his long, slow journey home, with the bundle going bump, bump, bump, along the ground behind him.

Suddenly he was pulled up short, and turning round, he saw that a large lizard had jumped on to the parcel of salt and was sitting there, staring at him.

'Get off my salt!' exclaimed Tortoise. 'How do you expect me to drag it home with you on top of it?'

'It's not your salt!' replied the lizard. 'I was just

walking along the path when I found this bundle lying there, so I took possession of it and now it belongs to me.'

'What rubbish you talk!' said Tortoise. 'You know very well it is mine, for I am holding the string that ties it.'

But the lizard still insisted that he had found the parcel lying in the road, and he refused to get off unless Tortoise went with him to the elders, to have their case tried in court. Poor Tortoise had to agree and together they went before the old men at the court.

First Tortoise put his case, explaining that as his arms and legs were so short he always had to carry bundles by dragging them along behind him.

Then the lizard put his side of the matter, saying that he had found the bundle lying in the road.

'Surely anything that is picked up on the road belongs to the one who picks it up?' cried the lizard.

The old men discussed the matter seriously for some time; but many of them were related to the lizard and thought that they might perhaps get a share of the salt, so eventually they decreed that the bundle should be cut into two, each animal taking half.

Tortoise was disappointed, because he knew it really was his salt, but he sighed with resignation and let them divide the parcel.

The lizard immediately seized the half that was covered with the biggest piece of cloth, leaving poor Tortoise with most of his salt escaping from his half of the parcel, and spilling out on to the ground. In vain did Tortoise try to gather his salt together. His hands were too small and there was too little cloth to wrap round it properly. Finally he departed for home, with only a fraction of his share, wrapped up in leaves and what remained of the bark cloth, while the elders scraped up all that had been spilled, dirty though it was, and took it back to their wives.

Tortoise's wife was very disappointed when she saw how little salt he had brought with him, and when he told her the whole story she was most indignant at the way he had been treated. The long, slow journey had tired him, and he had to rest for several days. But although Tortoise was so slow, he was very cunning and eventually thought up a plan to get even with the lizard.

So, saying goodbye to his wife, he plodded along the road towards the lizard's home with a gleam in his eye, and after some time he caught sight of the lizard, who was enjoying a solitary meal of flying ants. Slowly and silently Tortoise came upon him from behind and put his hands on the middle of the lizard's body.

'See what I've found!' called Tortoise loudly.

'What are you doing?' asked the perplexed lizard.

'I was just walking along the path when I found something lying there,' explained Tortoise. 'So I picked it up and now it belongs to me, just as you picked up my salt the other day.'

When the lizard continued to wriggle and demanded that Tortoise set him free, Tortoise insisted that they go to the court and get the elders to judge.

The old men listened attentively to both sides of the story, and then one said:

'If we are to be perfectly fair, we must give the same judgement that we gave concerning the salt.'

'Yes,' said the others, nodding their white heads, 'and we had the bag of salt cut in two. Therefore we must cut the lizard in two, and Tortoise shall have half.'

'That is fair,' replied Tortoise, and before the lizard could escape, he seized a knife from an elder's belt and sliced him in half. And that was the end of the greedy lizard.

The Rubber Man

S pider was a lazy fellow. The rainy season had come and everybody except Spider was working on the farms—hoeing, digging, and planting. Every morning Spider lay long in bed, only rising at mid-day, to eat a leisurely meal and spend the afternoon resting under a shady tree.

Now his wife knew that the other people in the village had almost finished their planting, and each day she would say hesitantly:

'Don't forget to tell me when you want my help on the farm,' for she dared say no more than that.

Spider would reply, 'Oh, there's plenty of time yet. The rains have scarcely begun.'

But as the days went by and people passing on the road called out to Spider, asking him when he was going to begin work on his farm, he decided on a plan.

'Today I shall begin clearing the weeds and tomorrow I shall plant ground-nuts,' he said to his wife one morning. 'Go to the market and buy a sackful, then roast them and salt them and have them ready for me to plant in the morning.'

'But husband,' objected his wife, 'whoever heard of ground-nuts being roasted and salted except for eating?'

'Don't argue with me, woman,' said Spider. 'I know what I am doing. Surely you understand that if we plant ground-nuts prepared in this way, then the fresh crop they produce will be already roasted and salted and we shall be able to eat them as soon as they are ripe, without cooking them at all.'

'How clever you are,' said his simple wife, as she set off for the market, while Spider went deep into the bush where no one could see him, and had a good sleep.

That evening Spider returned and told his wife how hard he had worked on the farm, while he watched her shelling, roasting, and salting the ground-nuts.

As soon as the sun rose, Spider took the sack of nuts and pretended to go to his farm. Along the little winding paths he went, until he was far away from the village and the farms. Then, sitting down beneath a tree, he had a wonderful feast and ate every single nut. He followed this with a drink of water from a nearby stream, then, curling up in the shade of a tree, slept soundly until sunset.

Hurrying home he called to his wife, 'Isn't supper ready yet? We men have a hard life! Here have I been working all day in the fields and you, with nothing to do except cook my supper, haven't even got it ready yet!'

'It's just coming,' replied his wife, as she brought him his meal. 'And I will put some water on the fire now, so that you can wash with warm water before you go to bed.'

Every day the same thing happened. Spider said goodbye to his wife in the morning and pretended to go to his farm, but instead of hoeing and weeding like the other men he found a quiet, lonely spot and went to sleep.

When evening came, he went back to his wife, complaining of his tired limbs and aching back, and after a well-cooked supper and a good wash he went to bed.

Time passed until, one by one, the other husbands began to bring home their harvest. But Spider brought nothing. At last his wife said:

'Surely our ground-nuts are ready by now? Nearly everyone in the village is harvesting.'

'Ours are slower than the others,' replied Spider. 'Wait a little longer.'

At last his wife changed her tactics and suggested:

'I'll come to the farm with you tomorrow and help with the harvest. I'm sure our nuts are ready now.'

'I don't want you working on the farm like a poor man's wife,' replied Spider. 'Have patience for a few more days and I'll harvest the ground-nuts myself and bring them home.'

Now Spider was indeed in a fix! How could he bring home ground-nuts to his wife when he had not even got a farm? There was only one solution. He must steal some.

That night, when his wife was asleep, he crept out of the house and made his way to the biggest farm of all, the chief's farm which still had row upon row of ground-nuts unharvested. As quietly as he could, he filled his leather bag with nuts which he dug from the ground, and hiding the bag in a tree some distance away, he returned home.

Early next morning he announced cheerfully to his wife:

'Aha! Today I go to the farm to harvest the first of our nuts. Mind you have a good supper waiting for me when I come home tired and weary.'

'Oh yes, husband, I will,' exclaimed his delighted wife, little knowing that Spider was going straight to the tree where he had hidden his bag and would sleep there all day. She had supper ready for him when he came home, complaining of exhaustion and describing how hard he had worked digging up the nuts, which he handed to her.

Joyfully she cracked open a nut and put it in her mouth. Then her face fell and she cried:

'But these are ordinary nuts! Did you not say that they would grow already roasted and salted?'

'I remember saying no such thing,' replied Spider. 'The reason we salted the nuts was to keep the ants from eating them, once I had planted them in the soil. What a stupid woman you are to think nuts can grow which are roasted and salted already!'

'I see,' said his wife. 'I must have misunderstood you,' and being a very simple woman she thought no more about it.

That night, and a number of following nights, Spider went back to the chief's farm, stole a bagful of ground-nuts and hid them in a tree. Then when morning came he pretended to go to his farm, had a long, deep sleep and returned to his wife with the stolen goods in the evening.

But alas! The chief's servant soon noticed that somebody was stealing his master's nuts and was determined to catch him, so taking several large calabashes, he went into the bush until he found some gutta-percha trees. Then, making long slashes in the bark, he left a calabash at the foot of each tree to catch the sap as it trickled out, and next day when he returned he found they were full of sticky, brown rubber. This he took back to the farm and made into the shape of a man which he placed in the middle of the chief's ground-nut field. Then he rubbed his hands together with glee and said to himself, 'Aha! Now I shall soon know who the thief is!'

When all was dark and the villagers were asleep in bed, Spider crept out of his house as usual and made his way silently to the chief's farm. He was just about to begin digging when he saw what he thought was the figure of a man, only a few yards away.

'Oh!' he gasped. 'What do you want here?' But there was no reply.

'Who are you?' Spider demanded a little louder. 'What are you doing on the chief's farm in the middle of the night?' But there was still no reply.

Spider became frightened and angry, so lifting his hand he struck the man a hard blow on the cheek, saying:

'Why don't you answer me?'

Now the rubber man had been standing in the sun all day and was still extremely sticky, and Spider found that he could not pull his hand away from the man's face.

'Let me go at once!' he spluttered. 'How dare you hold on to me like that!' And he hit him with the other hand. Now Spider really was in a fix as *both* hands were stuck, and he began to realize that this was no ordinary man. Lifting his knees he tried to free himself by pushing them against the man's body, only to find that they too were held fast.

Frantically he battered his head against the man's chest—and now he could not move at all!

'How foolish I am,' he said to himself. 'I shall have to stay here all night and everybody will know I am a thief.'

Sure enough when the morning came, the chief's servant hurried to the farm to see who had been caught. How he laughed when he saw Spider stuck to the rubber man—head, hands, knees and all.

21

'So you were the thief!' he exclaimed. 'I might have guessed it.'

Poor Spider! How ashamed he was when the chief's servant managed to get him away from the sticky rubber and brought him before the chief. For weeks afterwards he hid among the rafters of his house seeing and speaking to nobody, and ever since that day his descendants have always hidden in corners.

Tortoise and the Baboon

One evening when the tortoise was crawling slowly home, he met the baboon on his path.

'Hello, old fellow,' said the baboon heartily. 'Have you found much to eat today?'

'No,' replied Tortoise sadly. 'Very little indeed.'

The baboon danced up and down, chortling with laughter at an idea which had just come to him.

'Follow me, poor old Tortoise,' he exclaimed, 'and when you reach my home I will have supper all ready for you.'

'Thank you. Thank you,' said the grateful Tortoise, as the baboon turned round and bounced gaily along the path that led to his home.

Tortoise followed as fast as he could, which was very slow indeed, especially when he went uphill. Once or twice he stopped to rest, when the ground became so bumpy that he got disheartened, but holding in his mind the picture of a wonderful feast, he plodded on.

At last he reached the place in the bush that the baboon called his home. There he was, leaping about and grinning to himself, and as soon as he caught sight of Tortoise he exclaimed:

'Bless my tail! What a long time you have taken to get here. I declare it must be tomorrow already!'

'I'm so sorry,' said Tortoise, puffing a little after his long journey. 'But I'm sure you have had plenty of time to get the supper ready, so do not grumble at me.'

'Oh yes, indeed!' replied the baboon, rubbing his hands together. 'Supper's all ready. All you have to do is to climb up and get it. Look!' he said, pointing to the top of a tree. 'Three pots of millet-beer, brewed especially for you.'

The poor tortoise looked up at the pots which the baboon had wedged in the branches high above his head. He knew he could never reach them, and the baboon knew that too.

'Bring one down for me, there's a good friend,' begged Tortoise, but the baboon climbed the tree in the twinkling of an eye and shouted down to him:

'Oh no! Anybody who wants supper with me must climb up to get it.'

So poor Tortoise could only begin his long homeward journey with a very empty stomach, cursing at his inability to climb trees. But as he went he worked out a splendid plan for getting his own back on the unkind baboon.

A few days later the baboon had an invitation to eat with Tortoise. He was very surprised, but knowing how slow and good-natured the tortoise was, the baboon said to himself:

'Oh well! The fellow evidently saw the joke and bears me no malice. I'll go along and see what I can get out of him.'

At the appointed time the baboon set out along the track that led to Tortoise's home. Now it was the dry season, when many bush fires occur which leave the ground scorched and black. Just beyond the river the baboon found a wide stretch of burnt and blackened grass, over which he bounded towards Tortoise, who stood waiting beside a cooking pot from which issued the most savoury of smells.

'Ah, it's my friend the baboon!' said Tortoise. 'I'm very pleased to see you. But did your mother never teach you that you must wash your hands before meals? Just look at them! They're as black as soot.'

The baboon looked at his hands, which were indeed very black from crossing the burnt patch of ground.

'Now run back to the river and wash,' said Tortoise, 'and when you are clean I will give you some supper.'

The baboon scampered across the black earth and washed himself in the river, but when he came to return to Tortoise he found he had to cross the burnt ground again and so arrived as dirty as before.

'That will never do! I told you that you could only eat with me if you were clean. Go back and wash again! And you had better be quick about it because I have started my supper already,' said Tortoise, with his mouth full of food.

The poor baboon went back to the river time and again, but try as he would he got his hands and feet black each time he returned, and Tortoise refused to give him any of the delicious food that was fast disappearing. As Tortoise swallowed the last morsel, the baboon realized he had been tricked and with a cry of rage he crossed the burnt ground for the last time and ran all the way home.

'That will teach you a lesson, my friend,' said the Tortoise, smiling, as, well-fed and contented, he withdrew into his shell for a long night's sleep.

Spider and the Lion

One day Spider went to the river to fish. It must have been Spider's lucky day, for the fish swarmed around him until at last he had a large pile lying on the muddy bank beside him.

'Now for a fire to cook my supper,' exclaimed Spider in delight, and quickly collecting a few sticks, he made a fire and began roasting his fish.

As everybody knows, the smell of roasting fish is not only delicious but it travels quickly through the air, and so it happened that a passing lion stopped in his tracks, sniffed appreciatively once or twice and then followed his nose.

He found Spider just about to eat the first of the fish he had cooked, and roared, 'Give that to me,' so fiercely, that Spider handed it over without a word.

'Delicious!' exclaimed the lion, smacking his lips and half-closing his eyes, while he sat down beside the fire and said, 'Now cook me some more!'

Spider was too frightened of the large, fierce lion even to think of disobeying him and he certainly could not run away without abandoning all his fish. So he set to work to cook some more, hoping that the lion would soon have had enough and that there would be a few left for him. After all, he had done all the hard work and was aching with hunger.

One by one the savoury, sweet-smelling fish disappeared down the lion's throat while poor Spider was run off his feet collecting firewood. He got hotter and hotter as he stood over the fire, and sadder and sadder as he watched his pile of succulent fish getting smaller and smaller. In his despair the tears began to stream down his face and the lion laughed scornfully to see him weep.

'Ah no! I am not crying,' lied Spider proudly. 'It's the smoke from the fire making my eyes smart.'

As he said this he handed over the last of his precious fish to the lion, who swallowed it in one gulp without a word of thanks.

At that moment a beautiful brown bush-fowl ran past them and called out in surprise: 'Kuker! Kuker! Kuker!' Then she disappeared into the long grass and all was silent.

'Well, what do you think of that?' asked Spider. 'She didn't even pass the time of day with me. Never have I known such a rude and ungrateful bird. I expect she'll soon be telling her friends that it was not I who gave her her delicate spotted plumage.'

The lion looked up and asked: 'Did you say you gave her those spotted feathers?'

'Yes, of course I did,' replied Spider. 'Didn't you know that?'

The lion looked wistfully at his plain brown body and said, 'I should like a spotted skin too. Could you change mine for me?'

Spider half closed his eyes and looked critically at the

lion's fur. 'Well,' he said slowly and doubtfully, 'it would be a very difficult business.'

'Oh please do it for me,' begged the lion, rising to his feet. 'I could help you with the difficult part of it. Tell me what to do.'

Spider almost laughed with delight at how easily he had tricked the lion, but he managed to keep a serious face and replied:

'We need two things. First of all a big bush-cow, and then a well-grown kazaura tree.'

'I can soon get you the first,' said the lion. 'Wait here.'

Although the lion was so big, he slipped off into the bush without a sound, scarcely disturbing the grasses as he passed through them. For a long time all was quiet and Spider had nearly dropped asleep, when suddenly the lion re-appeared, dragging the body of a bush-cow with him.

'Now we must skin it,' explained Spider, 'for I need many strips of hide cut from the bush-cow's skin before I can make you as beautiful as the bush-fowl.'

The unsuspecting lion ripped the skin from the dead animal with his sharp claws, and then tore it into strips like pieces of rope.

'Splendid!' exclaimed Spider when he had finished. 'You've made a neat job of that. I should think that your spots will be far handsomer than the bush-fowl's.'

'Well, tell me what to do next,' said the lion impatiently.

'You must find me the toughest kazaura tree in the bush,' explained Spider. 'When you see a kazaura tree that you think will do, rush at it and knock into it with your chest. If it gives the slightest shake or seems to have weak roots, then that is no good. You must find a tree so

28

strong that it stands as firm as a rock when you knock into it.'

The lion tried several times and gave himself a number of bruises during the process, but at last he came upon a kazaura tree with such a thick trunk that it did not shake at all when he dashed into it.

Spider looked at the tree and pronounced it suitable and told the lion to go and fetch the strips of hide, and the bush-cow's carcass.

Meanwhile Spider collected a large pile of firewood and built another fire while the lion made a rack above it for roasting the meat.

'Now we come to the most difficult part of all,' declared Spider. 'You must lie down at the foot of this kazaura tree, and let me bind you tightly to it. The tighter you are bound, the better will be the final result.'

The foolish lion lay down and Spider began to truss him up with the leather thongs, until he could scarcely move, but the lion kept pointing out where the bonds were not tight enough, saying:

'It's loose here too,' and, 'I can still move my back legs. Surely you ought to tie them tighter than that!'

Spider could scarcely conceal his amusement as the stupid lion allowed himself to be tied up to the tree until he could not move at all. At last the lion cried:

'Well done! Nobody could tie me tighter than this. Now, let's get on with the spotting and then you can release me, for I don't want to stay like this longer than necessary.'

'Right!' exclaimed Spider triumphantly. 'You asked for it and now you shall have it.'

He put a number of metal skewers into the fire, and as soon as one became red-hot he would seize it and plunge it into the poor lion's skin, saying:

'That's in return for the first fish you ate. That's in return for the second. That's for the lovely fat perch which you swallowed, and that's for the eel that you stole.'

So he went on, branding the lion with the red-hot skewers and making brown marks all over his body.

'Now you are spotted like the bush-fowl,' jeered Spider, 'but you're mistaken if you think I am going to unbind you. There you can stay, until you die.'

The poor lion was frantic, but no amount of twisting and turning could undo his bonds; and to add insult to injury, Spider, seeing that the bush-cow was now nicely roasted, called all his family together and sat them down to feast before the very eyes of the helpless lion.

Night fell. Spider and his family went back to their home and the lion was left alone and helpless in the bush, where he lay for several days and nights. At last, just when he thought he must soon die for lack of food and water, a tiny white ant passed by, making but the faintest rustle as he walked over leaves and roots searching for food.

'Help me! Oh help me please, good little ant,' begged the lion.

The ant stopped in surprise and looked at him.

'What can a small creature like me do for a great animal like you?' it asked.

'You have such strong jaws,' replied the lion, 'that you could eat through these bonds in the twinkling of an eye. I have been here for days and am famished with hunger.'

The ant considered for a moment.

'If I set you free, then you would probably eat me up straightaway if you are as hungry as you say,' it replied.

'Certainly not,' expostulated the lion. 'Would I repay good with evil?'

'I think you would if you had the chance,' replied the ant. 'But I will help set you free all the same,' and it began to gnaw its way through the leather that tied the lion, until at last he was free. Carefully he stretched his cramped limbs and lay still until he had the strength to stand up and stagger away from the kazaura tree. He was ravenously hungry and would certainly have gobbled up the white ant had not that little creature already made good his escape.

Several days later when the lion had begun to recover and had managed to find a few small animals for food, he decided that Spider must be taught a lesson.

'Now where is that cunning Spider?' he roared. 'If I catch the villain I'll soon make short work of him,' and striding through the forest he loudly demanded of everyone he met, whether they had seen Spider.

Presently he saw a scrawny-looking gazelle in the distance and shouted to him: 'Have you seen Spider? I've a score to settle with him.'

The gazelle seemed to tremble as it answered, 'No. Allah be praised! I have not seen Spider, and should I see the evil creature I would hide immediately.'

'Surely you're not afraid of a mere spider?' asked the lion.

'Do you see how thin and wasted I have become?' said the gazelle. 'It is all the fault of that evil Spider. I quarrelled with him and in return he pointed his finger at me, cast a spell, and I wasted away.'

'How can that be?' asked the lion.

'I do not know,' replied the gazelle. 'But of one thing I am certain. If anybody displeases Spider, he does not

31

strike him. He just points his hand at him and he wastes away even as I am wasting away.'

The lion was terrified. He had no idea that Spider was so powerful.

'Then please do not tell him I was looking for him,' he begged, as he hurried away.

Now it was not a real gazelle. It was Spider inside an empty skin and it was he who had carried on the conversation with the lion. So he threw off the skin, and laughing heartily to himself, he followed the lion and caught him up.

'Somebody told me that you were looking for me,' he said arrogantly. 'Might I ask what you want?'

The lion threw himself down on the ground and prostrated himself before the spider.

'Oh no! Oh no indeed,' he stammered. 'You have been misinformed. I was not looking for you.'

'I should hope not,' said Spider. 'If I hear again that you are following me, you'll regret it as many another animal has done. And what's more, I am in charge of the bush now and all animals have to obey me, so don't you forget it!'

The frightened lion ran away as fast as he could, and from that day Spider was king of the animals and none dared to disobey him.

Thunder and Lightning

A long time ago, both thunder and lightning lived on this earth, among all the people. Thunder was an old mother sheep and Lightning was her son, a handsome ram, but neither animal was very popular.

When anybody offended the ram, Lightning, he would fly into a furious rage and begin burning down huts and corn bins, and even knock down large trees. Sometimes he damaged crops on the farms with his fire and occasionally he killed people who got in his way.

As soon as his mother, Thunder, knew he was behaving in this evil way, she would raise her voice and shout as loudly as she could, and that was very loud indeed.

Naturally the neighbours were very upset, first at the damage caused by Lightning and then by the unbearable noise that always followed his outbursts. The villagers complained to the king on many occasions, until at last he sent the two of them to live at the very edge of the village, and said that they must not come and mix with people any more.

However, this did no good, since Lightning could still see people as they walked about the village streets and so found it only too easy to continue picking quarrels with them. At last the king sent for them again.

'I have given you many chances to live a better life,' he said, 'but I can see that it is useless. From now on, you must go right away from our village and live in the wild bush. We do not want to see your faces here again.'

Thunder and Lightning had to obey the king and left the village, angrily cursing its inhabitants.

Alas, there was still plenty of trouble in store for the villagers, since Lightning was so angry at being banished that he now set fire to the whole bush, and during the dry season this was extremely unfortunate. The flames spread to the little farms which the people had planted, and sometimes to their houses as well, so that they were in despair again. They often heard the mother ram's mighty voice calling her son to order, but it made very little difference to his evil actions.

The king called all his councillors together and asked them to advise him, and at last they hit on a plan. One white-headed elder said:

'Why don't we banish Thunder and Lightning right away from the earth? Wherever they live there will be trouble, but if we sent them up into the sky, we should be rid of them.'

So Thunder and Lightning were sent away into the sky, where the people hoped they would not be able to do any more damage.

Things did not work out quite as well as they had hoped, however, for Lightning still loses his temper from time to time and cannot resist sending fire down to the earth when he is angry. Then you can hear his mother rebuking him in her loud rumbling voice.

Occasionally even his mother cannot bear to stay with him and goes away for a little while. You will know when this happens, for Lightning still flashes his fire on the earth, but his mother is so far away that she does not see, and her voice is silent.

Why the Crab has no Head or How the First River was Made

A long long time ago, when God made this earth, He chose the mighty elephant to be king of the world. The elephant and his subjects roamed through the dark green forests, and since there were no rivers in those days, God made a pond for them to drink from.

Now one day the elephant trumpeted loudly, and called for his friends the hawk and the crab.

'Tomorrow,' he announced, 'I am going hunting in the forest, and you must come with me.'

The hawk was overjoyed and flew away to get his bow and arrows, but the poor crab was a slow-moving creature and could not hold any hunting weapons. But he was determined not to be left out, so he crawled away to his home and began to think hard about the problem.

The next morning all three creatures met on the edge of the forest, and while the hawk and the elephant went off with their bows and arrows to a section of the forest where they knew they would find plenty of game, the crab

36

dragged a long net behind him, set it up in a spot he had chosen, and waited.

Presently a wounded animal rushed away from the elephant and the hawk, straight into the crab's net, and seizing a large piece of wood the crab quickly beat the animal on its head, so that it died at once.

This happened again and again. If the elephant or the hawk killed an animal outright, then they put it beside them for themselves, but if they only wounded one, the poor creature rushed away towards the crab's net. Once it was entangled there, the crab soon despatched it with his heavy stick, removed and hid the arrow that had wounded it, and put the carcass on his own pile.

By the afternoon, the elephant had killed five antelope and the hawk three, and each thought he had done very well.

'Let's go and find the crab,' suggested the elephant. 'I don't suppose the poor thing has managed to catch anything at all.'

How amazed they were to find the crab sitting proudly beside the carcasses of ten animals, all much bigger than himself. The hawk began congratulating him but the elephant was furious that the crab had killed more animals than he had, and shouted:

'Hawk! Kill that wretched crab. I, your king, order you to do so. Cut off his head at once!'

'Oh, sir! Oh, king!' begged the crab. 'Please do not kill me. I will give you all this meat and never come near you again if only you will let me live.'

At last the elephant consented, and seizing the crab's kill he bellowed:

'Go! Go! And never let me see you again.'

The crab sidled clumsily away, and hiding himself in

the thick undergrowth, once again gave himself up to deep thought, wondering how he could revenge himself on the elephant.

Presently he made his way to the elephant's home and crept up to the elephant's wife.

'Good woman,' he croaked, 'I have a message for you from our noble king, your husband. He says that the place where he has been hunting all day is very cold. You must make him some good soup with plenty of peppers in it to warm him up. Now don't forget! Plenty of peppers,' he repeated, and he hurried away as fast as he could.

The elephant's wife did as she was told, and flavoured the soup very strongly with peppers. No sooner had she finished cooking it than the elephant and the hawk came home from their hunting trip. They were both extremely hungry and began to eat the soup straight away.

Meanwhile the cunning crab made his way to the pond and began to fill it up with earth. He worked so hard that at last there was no water left at all, and feeling very satisfied with his evening's work, the crab dug a little hole in the middle of the place where the pond had been and hid himself there.

He had not long to wait. The hawk and the elephant finished up all the peppery soup and very naturally felt extremely thirsty.

'Let's go to the pond now,' suggested the elephant to his friend. 'I'm so thirsty, I could drink it quite dry.'

Of course, when they reached the pond it *was* quite dry and the two animals were angry and perplexed.

'What an extraordinary thing,' said the elephant. 'You must help me dig until we get down to the water again.'

So the two animals dug and dug, getting thirstier and more irritable every moment. Suddenly the elephant reached the hole where the crab was hidden, and as soon as he saw the crab he knew that it was he who had filled up the pond with earth.

'Ah ha!' he bellowed in a furious voice. 'It's no good begging for mercy this time!'

He seized the poor crab, cut off his head and threw him back into the mud.

Immediately the water started bubbling and gurgling up from below and soon the pond was nearly full again. The elephant and the hawk were delighted. They drank their fill and washed themselves, trumpeting and squawking with delight. They decided to leave the crab's body in the pond, as that seemed to be the cause of the water flowing again, and as they stood at the edge watching the water still rising rapidly, the elephant commanded:

'Dig an opening at the lower end of the pond, so that the water can run away. It's beginning to overflow.'

The hawk did as he was told, and sure enough, the water began to trickle out of the pond so that very soon a little stream was flowing. It got wider and wider and deeper and deeper until it became a big river, still flowing downhill.

Now the crab was not really dead, and soon realized that he could escape from the pond by way of the river. But the poor thing had no eyes since his head had been cut off, so he went to the mud-fish to see if he could do anything for him.

'I will do anything that I can,' replied the kindly fish, 'but I cannot give you any eyes. If you go to my friend the prawn, I think he could help you.'

Sure enough, the prawn could. He took some eyes and fastened them on to the crab's shoulders, since he had no head on which to put them.

The crab was delighted to be able to see again, and hurrying down the river he left the pond, the elephant, and the hawk far behind him.

So now you know how the first river started, and why the crab has no head.

A Test of Skill

Once there lived a chief who had three sons. They were fine, strong young men, and their father often wondered which of these gifted lads was the most clever.

One day when his councillors assembled in the Council Chamber, the chief looked around at the group of elderly men, shaking out their voluminous white robes as they settled down for a morning's discussion, and made up his mind to ask them to help him decide who was the cleverest of his three sons.

'Come over to this baobab tree,' he said, 'and let my three sons be brought here immediately.'

The old men rose to their feet, and moving out into the bright sunshine, they shuffled over the rough ground to the baobab tree.

After a few moments the three young men appeared, each leading a horse.

'My sons,' said the chief, 'I want each of you to mount your horse in turn and show your skill to all the people assembled here. You may do what you please, but when you reach this baobab tree, you must exert yourselves as never before and show us what you are made of.'

The three boys mounted their horses and galloped away from the chief, far up a dusty track which led to the wide courtyard of the chief's house.

A number of other people had joined the group of waiting councillors by now, and a murmur of anticipation rippled through the crowd as the first son was seen riding towards them in a cloud of dust.

Galloping furiously, the horseman made straight for the baobab tree, swerving neither to right nor left. Holding his spear aloft he plunged it into the trunk with such force that it made a great hole. Then to the amazement of the onlookers, the first of the chief's sons followed the spear and leapt through the hole on his horse, making a perfect landing on the ground beyond.

Those who were watching, shouted their applause.

'Surely,' they said, one to another, 'no one could do better than that.'

Then the second son came galloping towards them, his horse's hoofs beating a brisk tattoo on the dry ground. He appeared to ride straight at the tree, and carried no sword, so that the people thought he would dash himself to death against the tree.

But suddenly his horse rose in the air like an arrow and sailed right over the baobab, rider and horse landing unharmed on the other side.

The crowd laughed with pleasure and surprise and said one to another:

'Surely the third son will not be able to do better than this,' and they held their breath as the youngest son came riding towards them.

As he came level with the tree he seized its branches

42

in both hands, dug his spurs into his horse and wrenched the whole tree from the ground, roots and all. Then he rode up to his father, waving the tree aloft and smiling triumphantly as the crowd roared its applause.

Which of these three sons would you have chosen as the winner had you been the chief?

The Tale of the Superman

Once upon a time there was a man who believed he was stronger than anyone else in the whole world. He certainly was strong, for whenever he went to the forest to get firewood for his home, he would bring back a load ten times as big as most men could carry; and sometimes, when he found a dead tree lying on the ground, he would toss it on to his head with a mighty heave and carry it home in one piece. But he was proud too; and when he reached home, he would burst triumphantly into the compound, fling the load down on the ground, and call to his wife:

'Come and see what your superman has brought you!'

His wife would bend low as she came out of the door of her mud hut, then straighten her back and smile.

'Superman?' she would mock. 'If you really saw a superman you would run away from him. Don't talk to me of supermen! Strong you may be, but superman, no!'

Then the man would get angry and sit down under the cassia tree outside his hut muttering:

'It's a lie! I *am* a superman. Just show me another

44

who is stronger than I; then I will believe you when you say I am not a superman.'

One day the man's wife, whose name was Shetu, went to draw water. She took a large calabash, put it on her head, and walked along the winding bush path until she came to a well. Now this well was a magic one, and although Shetu managed to throw the bucket down into the water, she could not pull it up. She hauled and she tugged and she heaved; leaning backwards and digging her heels into the ground, she put her whole weight to the task. She even called upon Allah to help her, but all to no avail.

'Alas!' she exclaimed, sinking down on the mud beside the well and wiping the perspiration from her forehead with the hem of her skirt. 'Ten men would be needed to raise that bucket from the well today. I must go home without any water.'

Sadly she rose to her feet and began the journey back along the dusty path that wound in and out between the forest trees.

Suddenly she saw another woman approaching, and they stopped to exchange greetings.

'Why are you returning from the well with your calabash empty?' asked the stranger. 'Has the well dried up?'

'Oh no!' exclaimed Shetu. 'I have been struggling for a long time to raise the bucket from the water, but it is too heavy and I am not strong enough. It needs at least ten men to bring it to the top.'

The other woman smiled and said:

'Do not despair! Come, follow me to the well and I will see that you get your water after all.'

Shetu was sure that the woman would not be able to

45

help her, but decided to follow to prove the truth of her words. As the woman led the way back along the path, Shetu noticed a fine-looking baby tied on her back. He turned his head and stared at her with bright, unblinking eyes for so long that she began to feel uncomfortable under his gaze.

At length they reached the well, and Shetu showed the woman the long rope which stretched far down into the well, with the magic bucket on the end.

'See!' she began, 'I threw the bucket down but could not raise it up. I fear you will not be able to help either.'

The woman laughed, untied the child from her back, and told him to pull the bucket up from the well. Without faltering, the child seized the rope in his little fat hands and pulled the bucket up as easily as if it had been a feather on the end of a piece of string.

Shetu put her hand to her mouth in amazement. She could not speak, but the other woman did not seem at all disconcerted, and told her child to draw more water, which he did again and again, without any sign of strain.

The two women set to work, washing first themselves and then the clothes they were wearing. These soon dried in the hot sun. Then they filled their calabashes with water and began their homeward journey.

After a little while they came to a place where another path branched off to the east, and the woman with the baby turned up this new track.

'Where are you going?' asked Shetu.

'Home, of course,' replied the other.

'Is your home along that path?' said Shetu. 'I did not know that it led to a village. What is your husband's name?'

'My husband's name is Superman,' said the stranger; and walking quickly along the narrow track she soon disappeared into the forest.

Shetu was too amazed to speak, but as soon as she got back to her hut she told her husband all that had happened during the day.

At first he would not believe her, but soon he realized that she was speaking the truth, and anger welled up in him like bubbles rising in a pot of broth.

'Aha!' he exclaimed. 'So there is another man who calls himself a superman, is there? Just let me see him, that's all! I'll soon show him who is the real superman in these parts!'

'Oh no!' begged his wife. 'Keep away from him, in Allah's name, for I'm sure he will destroy you, and then what will become of me? If you had seen the strength of his infant son, you would realize that the father must be fifty times as strong.'

But nothing she could say would persuade her obstinate husband to give up his foolish idea.

'Early tomorrow morning,' he said firmly, 'you must take me to the path that leads to this man's house.'

So next day the husband got up before dawn and, full of confidence, took his hunting weapons from their hiding-place. With a quiver of sharp arrows on his back, his bow in his hand, and his trusty sword slung from his shoulder, he felt ready for anything.

Then he shouted to his terrified wife:

'Come along, lazy-bones! Come out of that hut and lead me to the place where this impostor lives! No, wait!' he exclaimed. 'First of all take me to this magic well, that I may see the bucket for myself.'

The woman picked up her calabash, placed it on her

47

head, and led the way to the well. She was far too worried to realize how foolish it was to take a vessel to a well from which neither of them would be able to draw water; but she hurried along the path, with her husband still shouting at her from the rear. Presently she noticed that there was another figure on the path in front, and when she and her husband reached the well, they found the other woman and her baby son were there too.

Shetu greeted them, but her husband ignored them and began to peer down into the well, straining his eyes to catch sight of the water at the bottom.

'Give me that bucket!' he stormed, and snatching it from the ground beside the well he threw it with all his strength down into the dark cavity, where they all heard it strike the water with a resounding splash.

'I'll put paid to this nonsense once and for all,' he boasted, as he began to haul on the rope. 'Ten men, indeed! Watch me pull the bucket up!'

He grunted and groaned, he swore and he sweated, but the bucket would not come up. Frustrated, he leaned further and further into the well, cursing the bucket, the rope and the water so heartily that he forgot to keep his foot anchored against the rim of the well, and all but tumbled in after the bucket.

Just in time the baby boy reached his hand over the cloth that tied him to his mother's back, seized both the rope and the man, and whisked man and bucket safely out of the well with never a word.

The man sat on the ground in dazed surprise, rubbing his head and watching the child, who had clambered down from his mother's back, pull up bucket after bucket of cold, clear water, while his mother filled her water-pot.

Then Shetu turned to him triumphantly.

'Now that you have seen what the son of the real superman can do, are you not afraid to meet the superman himself?'

The man had been silently wondering how he could get out of his visit to the real superman's compound; but since his wife had shamed him by suggesting he would be afraid, he had to put a brave face on things. So he said stubbornly, still rubbing his bruised head:

'I am more determined than ever to go and see this so-called superman.'

'Right! Then you go alone,' said Shetu, and, seizing her calabash which the child had filled with water, she placed it on her head and hurried away from the well.

The other woman turned doubtfully to the man.

'So you want to see my husband, do you?' she asked. 'You'd be far better off if you went home.' But he would not listen, and presently the woman fastened her baby on her back again and led the way through the forest.

At last they reached the woman's compound. It looked much the same as any other home, and there was nothing to show that it belonged to a superman, so the man's courage began to return.

'My husband, the superman, is away hunting in the forest,' explained the woman. 'You can hide somewhere until he comes back, and then you can peep out and look at him. But do not let him see you. He eats men like you!'

'Bah!' said the man, 'I'm not afraid. There's no need for me to hide.'

'What if I tell you that my husband ate a whole elephant for breakfast today, and has been known to eat ten elephants at one sitting?' asked the woman. 'Are you not then afraid, O foolish little man?'

So the man let her lead him to a corn bin that stood on the edge of the compound. It was made of mud, and looked rather like an outsized water-pot, and when the man had climbed in through the opening at the top, he found he could see over the edge only by standing on tiptoe.

'Now keep quiet, if you value your life,' admonished the woman as she left him. 'I must cook my husband's supper.'

Towards evening the man in the corn bin heard a sound like an approaching tornado. A great wind began to shake the forest trees, and to lift the thatch from the nearby huts. Then into the clearing around the compound came the master of the house. As he spoke, the air throbbed with the power of his voice, and his feet shook the ground like an earthquake.

'Wife! Wife!' he called. 'Have you cooked me my elephant?'

'Indeed I have,' replied the woman. 'Come and see whether this one is big enough for your supper.'

The man in the corn bin cowered with fright. So it was true! There was, after all, another more worthy of the name of Superman. How he did hope with all his heart that the elephant the woman had cooked was big enough. He stood trembling while he heard the superman eating his supper and cracking elephant bones like sticks of sugar-cane.

'Allah grant that the elephant is a big one,' he murmured again and again between his chattering teeth.

Time passed until, when the sky was dark and night had come, the real superman began to shout:

'Wife! Wife! I smell the smell of a man. Where is he, that I may eat him?'

'Good husband, I am the one whom you can smell,' she replied. 'There is no one here but me.' But she found it difficult to satisfy her husband that there was no one hidden in the compound. He prowled about, shaking the place with his shouts and heavy footsteps, while the man in the corn bin nearly died of fright.

At last the superman left the compound and began to search in the nearby forest land, roaring all the while:

'I smell the smell of a man.'

As soon as he was gone, the woman crept over to the corn bin and whispered to the terrified man within:

'Oh, why did you not believe me from the first? What a lot of trouble we should both have been saved.'

'Alas! I am truly sorry,' said the foolish man. 'But how could I believe such a thing unless I saw it with my own eyes? And how can I escape from this place?'

'Now listen,' whispered the woman. 'Soon my husband will return for the night. Watch the door of our hut, and when my husband is fast asleep I will put my little lamp outside. Then you must make haste and escape, and never come back here again.'

'Thank you! Thank you!' said the man, trembling violently as he felt the wind blow across the compound, heralding the return of the superman.

The hours passed slowly, but the man dared not sleep. Then at last, just before dawn, he saw a tiny flickering light, like a fire-fly, at the door of the hut. Carefully he swung himself up on to the rim of the corn bin and let himself down to the ground without a sound. Then he began to run. And how he did run! Never had his feet taken such long strides, or his heart beat so quickly.

Just when he thought he was safe, he heard the roars

of the superman in the distance, and his heart sank, while he felt sick with fright.

'I smell the smell of a man,' shouted the voice he had learnt to dread.

The poor man ran faster and faster, until he came to a field where some men were clearing the ground to make a farm. They stopped in their task of uprooting bushes and felling trees and enquired:

'Hey! Where are you going? Who is chasing you, that you run so fast?'

'Someone who calls himself Superman is chasing me,' panted the runner. 'Can you help me?'

'There are several of us here,' replied the men. 'Stay with us until this so-called superman catches you up, and we'll deal with him.'

The man crouched panting on the ground, when suddenly a mighty wind rose up so strong that it lifted all the labourers off the ground and dropped them several yards away.

'Here!' they called in fright. 'What's happening to us?'

'It's that superman,' exclaimed the terrified fugitive. 'He puffs and blows so strongly that a great wind precedes him.'

'If that's the case, we are no match for him,' said the men, now terrified in their turn. 'You'd better keep on running.'

So the man leapt to his feet in fear, and began his race again. Presently he came to another group of men, who were hoeing up the ground in preparation for planting. They straightened up, and looked at him in amazement.

'Hey! Where are you going? Who is chasing you, that you run so fast?' they shouted.

'Someone who calls himself Superman is chasing me,' puffed the man. 'Can you help me?'

The men laughed. 'There are ten of us here,' they said. 'Surely we can deal with your so-called superman. Stay with us until he catches you up.'

The man collapsed gratefully on to a heap of earth and tried to get his breath back. Then the men who were hoeing found themselves being blown about by a strong wind, which tumbled them higgledy-piggledy all over their farm.

'Here!' they said. 'What's happening to us?'

'It's that superman,' said the man despondently. 'He puffs and he blows so strongly that a great wind precedes him.'

'In that case, we are no match for such a man,' said the men who had been hoeing. 'You'd better keep on running.' And they lay flat on their faces, hoping that the superman would not see them as he passed by.

By now the poor man was nearly dead with fatigue, but with a great effort he managed to drag himself to his feet and continued to run away from the superman, even faster than before.

Presently he came to another group of men, who were planting guinea corn seed in a patch of ground already cleared and hoed.

'Hey! Where are you going?' they called in surprise. 'Who is chasing you, that you run so fast?'

'Someone who calls himself Superman is chasing me,' replied the poor fellow in a weak voice. 'Can you help me?'

'Well, there are a dozen or more of us here,' replied one of the men. 'I don't think a superman would bother *us* much. Stay with us until he catches you up.'

The man staggered and fell, too exhausted to say more, but after a few moments a mighty wind came. It lifted up the men who were sowing, whirled them round in the air, and cast them to the ground in a heap.

'Here!' they gasped. 'What's happening to us?'

'It's that superman,' explained the runner in despair, knowing full well what would be the outcome.

'Then you'd better keep on running,' said the frightened men, as they dropped their long planting hoes and handfuls of seed and ran helter-skelter into the forest to hide.

The man thought his end had come, but rousing himself to make one last effort, he ran on. Suddenly, as he rounded a bend in the path, he saw in the distance what looked like a huge man sitting under a baobab tree, his enormous legs stretched out beside the path.

'I've dodged a wasp, only to run into a hornet,' he thought, as he tried to hide behind a bush. 'But no! nothing can be worse than the fate which will befall me if I stop running.'

So he went on his way, with his heart in his mouth.

When he reached the baobab tree, he found that it was indeed a gigantic man sitting there, surrounded by roasted elephants which he was hungrily eating, and throwing their huge bones away over his shoulder into the forest.

'Stop!' he boomed. 'Who is chasing you, that you run so fast?'

The exhausted man fell in a heap at the giant's feet, and panted:

'Someone who calls himself Superman is chasing me. Can you help me?'

'Of course I can,' boomed the giant. 'I am Giant-of-the-Forest. Stay with me until he catches you up.'

Suddenly the wind made by the puffings and blowings of the superman lifted our poor man from the ground and twirled him round and round in the air. Then he fell down some distance away from the giant.

'Come back,' called Giant-of-the-Forest. 'Don't you want me to help you?'

'I couldn't stop myself,' explained the man. 'It's the breath of that superman.'

But the giant did not seem at all put out. He laughed kindly and said, 'Give me your hand. I will sit on it, and then the breath of this so-called superman cannot blow you away.'

There they sat—and the man's arm was almost crushed by the weight of the giant—until Superman came rushing up to them. He was in a fine temper!

'Give me that man,' he bellowed to the giant. 'He's mine! I want to eat him.'

'Come and take him then,' said the giant, grinning horribly.

Then Superman leapt at the giant, who rose to his feet and began to fight with him. They leapt, they stamped, they struggled and wrestled, twisting their legs together, each trying to throw the other to the ground. Then, with a mighty leap, they endeavoured to loosen each other's grip. So mighty was the leap that they rose together far into the heavens and disappeared from sight.

The man could not believe his luck at first, but he soon came to his senses, slipped quietly into the forest, and began another long race to his home.

When he got back, his wife was delighted to see him, for she had never expected to set eyes on him again. He told her all about his alarming adventures, trying to show himself in the light of a hero. But his wife would have none of it.

'Let that be a lesson to you,' she said callously. 'Never boast about your achievements again. However strong or clever or rich or powerful you are, there is always somebody more so.'

And the man had to admit that she was right.

As for the real Superman and Giant-of-the-Forest, to this day they are still up there wrestling in the heavens. When they are tired they sit on a cloud to recover their strength, but soon they rise up again and continue the struggle. And if you listen carefully you will sometimes hear them fighting. People may tell you it is thunder, but you will know it is really Superman and Giant-of-the-Forest wrestling high above the clouds.

Why the Bush-Fowl Calls at Dawn and Why Flies Buzz

One day a man and his wife went into the bush to collect nuts. They found a palm tree with clusters of ripe nuts growing among the large green leaves, and telling his wife to wait below, the man soon climbed to the top of the tree, with his knife in his belt.

He was hacking away at the heavy clusters of palm nuts when a small black fly buzzed round his face, tickling his nose and trying to get into the corner of his eye. As he hastily brushed it away, his hand slipped and the knife began to fall.

'Wife!' he called. 'Move away! The knife is falling.'

The woman quickly leapt aside so that the knife missed her, but as she did so she jumped over a snake which was sleeping under the dead leaves. This so frightened the snake that it dived into the nearest place of refuge it could see, which happened to be a rat's hole.

The poor rat was terrified, and dashing past the snake he managed to get out of his hole and ran up the nearest tree for safety.

Unfortunately the rat had chosen a tree where the plantain-eater bird had built her nest, and thinking that the rat was after her eggs, she set up such a cackling and a screaming that the monkey in another tree was almost frightened out of his wits. He had been just about to eat a nice juicy mango which he had picked, but in his terror he dropped it.

The mango fell with a thud on to the back of an elephant who was walking quietly below, minding his own business. Imagining that he was being attacked by hunters he rushed madly away, catching his head in a flowering creeper which was climbing up a tree and dragging it through the bush in his flight.

The creeper had a strong stem which became entwined round a tall earthen ant heap, pulling it to the ground, where it fell on to a nest full of bush-fowl's eggs and broke them all.

'Kark!' squawked the poor mother bush-fowl. 'Look what you've done to my eggs,' and spreading her feathers over the ruined nest she collapsed in misery and uttered not another sound for two whole days and nights.

Now everyone knows that the bush-fowl is always the first to wake among the wild creatures, and that when the sun hears her loud and raucous cries, he rises from his bed and a new day begins. But since the bush-fowl was silently brooding over her loss, she had not called the sun, and the sky remained dark. The other animals wondered why the daylight did not come, and cried out to the Great Spirit of the Heavens, asking him what had happened.

So the Great Spirit summoned all the animals together, and even the bush-fowl had to answer his call.

'Why have you not wakened the sun these last two

mornings?' the Spirit asked the bush-fowl, who stood before all the other animals and answered:

> 'My eggs were broken by the falling ant heap which
>   was pulled over by the creeper,
> Which was dragged down by the elephant,
> Who was hit by a mango,
> Which was dropped by a monkey,
> Who was startled by a bird,
> Who was frightened by a rat,
> Who was scared by a serpent,
> Who was wakened by a woman,
> Who was running from a knife,
> Which was dropped by her husband,
> Who was tickled by a black fly
> Up a palm tree.'

So the Great Spirit turned to the ant heap and asked: 'Why were you so careless as to fall and break the bush-fowl's eggs?'

The ant heap, which had by now collected itself together, replied:

> 'I was pulled over by the creeper,
> Which was dragged down by the elephant,
> Who was hit by a mango,
> Which was dropped by a monkey,
> Who was startled by a bird,
> Who was frightened by a rat,
> Who was scared by a serpent,
> Who was wakened by a woman,
> Who was running from a knife,
> Which was dropped by her husband,

> *Who was tickled by a black fly*
> *Up a palm tree.'*

Then the Great Spirit said to the flowering creeper: 'Why were you so careless as to pull over the ant heap?'

So the creeper replied:

> *'I was dragged down by the elephant,*
> *Who was hit by a mango,*
> *Which was dropped by a monkey,*
> *Who was startled by a bird,*
> *Who was frightened by a rat,*
> *Who was scared by a serpent,*
> *Who was wakened by a woman,*
> *Who was running from a knife,*
> *Which was dropped by her husband,*
> *Who was tickled by a black fly*
> *Up a palm tree.'*

The Great Spirit turned to the elephant. 'Why were you so careless as to pull down the flowering creeper?' he asked.

The elephant answered:

> *'I was hit by a mango,*
> *Which was dropped by a monkey,*
> *Who was startled by a bird,*
> *Who was frightened by a rat,*
> *Who was scared by a serpent,*
> *Who was wakened by a woman,*
> *Who was running from a knife,*
> *Which was dropped by her husband,*
> *Who was tickled by a black fly*
> *Up a palm tree.'*

The mango was still lying on the ground where it had bounced off the elephant's back, so the Great Spirit asked it why it had fallen so heavily and frightened the big creature.

> *'I was dropped by a monkey,*
> *Who was startled by a bird,*
> *Who was frightened by a rat,*
> *Who was scared by a serpent,*
> *Who was wakened by a woman,*
> *Who was running from a knife,*
> *Which was dropped by her husband,*
> *Who was tickled by a black fly*
> *Up a palm tree,'*

replied the mango.

'That was very careless of you, Monkey,' said the Great Spirit. So the monkey chattered and said:

> *'I was startled by a bird,*
> *Who was frightened by a rat,*
> *Who was scared by a serpent,*
> *Who was wakened by a woman,*
> *Who was running from a knife,*
> *Which was dropped by her husband,*
> *Who was tickled by a black fly*
> *Up a palm tree.'*

'And what have you to say for yourself?' the Great Spirit asked the bird, who replied:

> *'I was frightened by a rat,*
> *Who was scared by a serpent,*

> *Who was wakened by a woman,*
> *Who was running from a knife,*
> *Which was dropped by her husband,*
> *Who was tickled by a black fly*
> *Up a palm tree.'*

'Rat! Rat! Why did you frighten the plantain-eating bird?' asked the Great Spirit.

> *'I was scared by a serpent,*
> *Who was wakened by a woman,*
> *Who was running from a knife,*
> *Which was dropped by her husband,*
> *Who was tickled by a black fly*
> *Up a palm tree,'*

said the rat.

Then the Great Spirit called upon the snake to explain why he had alarmed the rat.

> *'I was wakened by a woman,*
> *Who was running from a knife,*
> *Which was dropped by her husband,*
> *Who was tickled by a black fly*
> *Up a palm tree,'*

replied the snake.

'Woman! Come here and tell me why you wakened the serpent,' commanded the Great Spirit, and the woman explained:

> *'I was running from a knife,*
> *Which was dropped by my husband,*

> *Who was tickled by a black fly*
> *Up a palm tree.'*

'Then the knife must explain why he made you run,' said the Great Spirit, and a little voice piped up from the man's belt, saying:

> *'I was dropped by her husband,*
> *Who was tickled by a black fly*
> *Up a palm tree.'*

'It is a dangerous thing to drop knives,' said the Great Spirit to the man. 'Why did you do so?'

> *'I was tickled by a black fly*
> *Up a palm tree,'*

replied the man.

'Then it seems to me,' said the Great Spirit, 'that all this trouble was caused by the black fly. Why did you tickle the man's face while he was up the palm tree, O black fly?'

But instead of answering courteously, as the others had done, the black fly flew about their heads and would only say, 'Buzz! Buzz! Buzz!'

The Great Spirit repeated his question, and again the only answer he got was 'Buzz! Buzz! Buzz!' for the fly refused to say a word. Then the Great Spirit was angry, and exclaimed:

'Because you have refused to answer my questions, I have taken away your power of speech. From now onwards, you will only be able to buzz.'

Then turning to the bush-fowl, the Great Spirit said:

'Never again must you neglect to call the sun at dawn, whatever may have happened to your eggs.'

The bush-fowl hung her head and promised she would never forget, and, as you know, she never has. Neither has the black fly ever got back his voice and you can still hear him and his brothers flying about the world saying nothing but 'Buzz! Buzz! Buzz!'

Spider and Squirrel

O nce upon a time there lived a squirrel who was a very fine farmer. In those days every animal had a large plot of land on which he grew his crops, and at the time when this story begins, Squirrel had a fine big field of guinea corn.

Now since Squirrel was such an adept at climbing trees and leaping from branch to branch, he never had to make a path to his plot of land. He simply chose a likely piece of bush and no matter how far it was from the road, he could always reach it through the tops of the trees.

Squirrel was delighted with this particular field. The soil was so rich that his guinea corn promised to be the best in the neighbourhood and he was rightly proud of the results of his labour.

One day when Squirrel's corn was almost ready for harvesting, Spider was out hunting in that part of the country and came across the field full of the finest-looking guinea corn he had ever seen.

'I wonder whose field this is?' said Spider to himself, as he walked round and round the field looking for the path that he hoped would lead him to the owner's house. But, of course, he could not find one.

'Well, this is a strange thing. How can anybody have a field with no path to it? I must look into this and see if I can profit by it.'

All the way back to his home and family, Spider considered how he could convince other people that the field belonged to him, and that evening after supper he had an idea.

'Tomorrow,' he said to his family, who were clustered around him, 'you must all come with me to a place I have discovered, and if you work hard for only one day, then you will be rewarded with a whole field of corn for which anyone else would need to work for months.'

He explained to his family what he wanted them to do, and very early the next day Spider and his children were at work with their hoes making a path through the bush leading to Squirrel's farm. When this was done the crafty spiders broke pieces of pottery and scattered them along the path, so that it would appear that they had dropped them over a period of several weeks as they went daily to hoe and weed.

Then, without a word to poor Squirrel, the spider family began to cut down the corn and take it home with them. Each morning they came back for a little more and spent the rest of the day eating and resting.

Squirrel soon discovered that he was being robbed, and one morning he hid himself in the trees, waiting to see who was stealing his corn. Along came Spider and his family and no sooner had they begun to cut down the guinea corn than Squirrel leapt out of his hiding-place.

'Why are you stealing my corn?' he asked.

'It is my corn,' replied Spider. 'Why are you trespassing on my field?'

'It is my field,' said the angry Squirrel.

Spider laughed.

'Oh no!' he said. 'It cannot be your field, for there is no path leading to it except the one that my family and I made.'

'But I do not need a path,' explained Squirrel. 'I always come by the treetops.'

Spider went on laughing, while his family continued to cut down Squirrel's harvest, so Squirrel cried:

'I shall go to court about this, you thieves! I dug this field and planted and weeded it, and I am not going to stand by and watch you steal it from me.'

So Squirrel went to court and Spider was sent for to state his case.

'Of course the field is mine,' said Spider to the judge. 'Have you ever seen a field with no path leading to it through the bush?'

The judge had to admit that all the fields he had seen had paths leading to them and when Spider showed him the path he had made and Squirrel admitted that the path was not his, the judge ruled that the field belonged to Spider and his children.

They all danced and shouted with glee and decided to work very hard the next day, to cut down the whole of the remaining harvest and take it home to store. So the next morning poor Squirrel had to watch the Spider family reaping the harvest over which he had toiled for so long. They tied the corn into great bundles and when all was cut, they started off for home staggering under their great loads.

Suddenly a great storm arose. The sky was black with

clouds and the rain beat down so heavily that Spider and his family had to leave their bundles of guinea corn at the road-side and dash to shelter in a disused hut. It was the worst storm they had had for a long time, and when the sky finally cleared and the sun shone again they made their way back along the steaming ground to the path where they had left their bundles of corn. Then they stood still and gazed in surprise at a gigantic black crow who was perched on the corn with outstretched wings.

So great was the crow that by spreading his wings he had kept the rain from falling on the bundles of guinea corn, and it was quite dry.

Spider was delighted.

'Thank you, Crow. Thank you!' he said happily. 'You have kept my corn dry and now I shall not have to spread it all out in the sun again.'

'*Your* corn?' objected the crow. 'It's my corn now. Who ever heard of anyone leaving bundles of corn unattended by the side of the path. Go away! This belongs to me.'

Then the crow gathered up all the corn in his huge claws, and flew away out of sight. So there was nothing left for Spider and his family to do except to return home empty-handed and very angry.

You might think that Spider would have learnt a lesson from this, and would have given up his thieving ways, but I am sorry to say that in no time at all he forgot about it and was soon up to his tricks again.

Unanana and the Elephant

M any, many years ago there was a woman called
Unanana who had two beautiful children. They
lived in a hut near the roadside and people
passing by would often stop when they saw the children,
exclaiming at the roundness of their limbs, the smoothness
of their skin, and the brightness of their eyes.

Early one morning Unanana went into the bush to
collect firewood and left her two children playing with a
little cousin who was living with them. The children
shouted happily, seeing who could jump the furthest, and
when they were tired they sat on the dusty ground outside
the hut, playing a game with pebbles.

Suddenly they heard a rustle in the nearby grasses,
and seated on a rock they saw a puzzled-looking baboon.

'Whose children are those?' he asked the little cousin.

'They belong to Unanana,' she replied.

'Well, well, well!' exclaimed the baboon in his deep
voice. 'Never have I seen such beautiful children before.'

Then he disappeared and the children went on with
their game.

A little later they heard the faint crack of a twig and

looking up they saw the big, brown eyes of a gazelle staring at them from beside a bush.

'Whose children are those?' she asked the cousin.

'They belong to Unanana,' she replied.

'Well, well, well!' exclaimed the gazelle in her soft, smooth voice. 'Never have I seen such beautiful children before,' and with a graceful bound she disappeared into the bush.

The children grew tired of their game, and taking a small gourd they dipped it in turn into the big pot full of water which stood at the door of their hut, and drank their fill.

A sharp bark made the cousin drop her gourd in fear when she looked up and saw the spotted body and treacherous eyes of a leopard, who had crept silently out of the bush.

'Whose children are those?' he demanded.

'They belong to Unanana,' she replied in a shaky voice, slowly backing towards the door of the hut in case the leopard should spring at her. But he was not interested in a meal just then.

'Never have I seen such beautiful children before,' he exclaimed, and with a flick of his tail he melted away into the bush.

The children were afraid of all these animals who kept asking questions and called loudly to Unanana to return, but instead of their mother, a huge elephant with only one tusk lumbered out of the bush and stood staring at the three children, who were too frightened to move.

'Whose children are those?' he bellowed at the little cousin, waving his trunk in the direction of the two beautiful children who were trying to hide behind a large stone.

'They . . . they belong to Una . . . Unanana,' faltered the little girl.

The elephant took a step forward.

'Never have I seen such beautiful children before,' he boomed. 'I will take them away with me,' and opening wide his mouth he swallowed both children at a gulp.

The little cousin screamed in terror and dashed into the hut, and from the gloom and safety inside it she heard the elephant's heavy footsteps growing fainter and fainter as he went back into the bush.

It was not until much later that Unanana returned, carrying a large bundle of wood on her head. The little girl rushed out of the house in a dreadful state and it was some time before Unanana could get the whole story from her.

'Alas! Alas!' said the mother. 'Did he swallow them whole? Do you think they might still be alive inside the elephant's stomach?'

'I cannot tell,' said the child, and she began to cry even louder than before.

'Well,' said Unanana sensibly, 'there's only one thing to do. I must go into the bush and ask all the animals whether they have seen an elephant with only one tusk. But first of all I must make preparations.'

She took a pot and cooked a lot of beans in it until they were soft and ready to eat. Then seizing her large knife and putting the pot of food on her head, she told her little niece to look after the hut until she returned, and set off into the bush to search for the elephant.

Unanana soon found the tracks of the huge beast and followed them for some distance, but the elephant himself was nowhere to be seen. Presently, as she passed through some tall, shady trees, she met the baboon.

'O baboon! Do help me!' she begged. 'Have you seen an elephant with only one tusk? He has eaten both my children and I must find him.'

'Go straight along this track until you come to a place where there are high trees and white stones. There you will find the elephant,' said the baboon.

So the woman went on along the dusty track for a very long time but she saw no sign of the elephant.

Suddenly she noticed a gazelle leaping across her path.

'O gazelle! Do help me! Have you seen an elephant with only one tusk?' she asked. 'He has eaten both my children and I must find him.'

'Go straight along this track until you come to a place where there are high trees and white stones. There you will find the elephant,' said the gazelle, as she bounded away.

'Oh dear!' sighed Unanana. 'It seems a very long way and I am so tired and hungry.'

But she did not eat the food she carried, since that was for her children when she found them.

On and on she went, until rounding a bend in the track she saw a leopard sitting outside his cave-home, washing himself with his tongue.

'O leopard!' she exclaimed in a tired voice. 'Do help me! Have you seen an elephant with only one tusk? He has eaten both my children and I must find him.'

'Go straight along this track until you come to a place where there are high trees and white stones. There you will find the elephant,' replied the leopard, as he bent his head and continued his toilet.

'Alas!' gasped Unanana to herself. 'If I do not find this place soon, my legs will carry me no further.'

She staggered on a little further until suddenly, ahead of her, she saw some high trees with large white stones spread about on the ground below them.

'At last!' she exclaimed, and hurrying forward she found a huge elephant lying contentedly in the shade of the trees. One glance was enough to show her that he had only one tusk, so going up as close as she dared, she shouted angrily:

'Elephant! Elephant! Are you the one that has eaten my children?'

'Oh no!' he replied lazily. 'Go straight along this track until you come to a place where there are high trees and white stones. There you will find the elephant.'

But the woman was sure this was the elephant she sought, and stamping her foot, she screamed at him again:

'Elephant! Elephant! Are you the one that has eaten my children?'

'Oh no! Go straight along this track—' began the elephant again, but he was cut short by Unanana who rushed up to him waving her knife and yelling:

'Where are my children? Where are they?'

Then the elephant opened his mouth and without even troubling to stand up, he swallowed Unanana with the cooking-pot and her knife at one gulp. And this was just what Unanana had hoped for.

Down, down, down she went in the darkness, until she reached the elephant's stomach. What a sight met her eyes! The walls of the elephant's stomach were like a range of hills, and camped among these hills were little groups of people, many dogs and goats and cows, and her own two beautiful children.

'Mother! Mother!' they cried when they saw her. 'How did you get here? Oh, we are so hungry.'

Unanana took the cooking-pot off her head and began to feed her children with the beans, which they ate ravenously. All the other people crowded round, begging for just a small portion of the food, so Unanana said to them scornfully:

'Why do you not roast meat for yourselves, seeing that you are surrounded by it?'

She took her knife and cut large pieces of flesh from the elephant and roasted them over a fire she built in the middle of the elephant's stomach, and soon everyone, including the dogs and goats and cattle, was feasting on elephant-meat very happily.

But the groans of the poor elephant could be heard all over the bush, and he said to those animals who came along to find out the cause of his unhappiness:

'I don't know why it is, but ever since I swallowed that woman called Unanana, I have felt most uncomfortable and unsettled inside.'

The pain got worse and worse, until with a final grunt the elephant dropped dead. Then Unanana seized her knife again and hacked a doorway between the elephant's ribs through which soon streamed a line of dogs, goats, cows, men, women, and children, all blinking their eyes in the strong sunlight and shouting for joy at being free once more.

The animals barked, bleated or mooed their thanks, while the human beings gave Unanana all kinds of presents in gratitude to her for setting them free, so that when Unanana and her two children reached home, they were no longer poor.

The little cousin was delighted to see them, for she had thought they were all dead, and that night they had a feast. Can you guess what they ate? Yes, roasted elephant-meat.

Spider's Web

The animals were lonely. They stood in the forest talking to one another, wondering how they could each get a wife to keep them company and to cook their food for them.

When Hare joined the group, he was soon able to tell them what to do.

'I have heard that there are plenty of wives up in the sky, beyond the clouds,' he said.

'But how shall we get there?' they asked.

'I will spin a strong web and fasten it on to a cloud,' said Spider, 'and then you will be able to climb up it, and find wives.'

So Spider began to spin, and very soon he was lost to sight high above them all with only the ladder of silver thread to show them the way he had gone. Presently Hare declared that all was ready and, leading the way, he began to climb up into the sky followed by all the other animals.

How the silken thread trembled as the elephant, the buffalo, the lion, and the monkey climbed higher and higher, while Hare turned back from time to time, urging them onwards.

At last they reached the country above the clouds and began to bargain for wives with the people there. Hare had been quite right when he said there were plenty of wives to be had, and soon most of the animals had chosen a wife and paid the agreed dowry.

Not so Hare. He chose his wife and made some excuse to her mother so that he did not pay the price immediately. Then he crept round the back of his future mother-in-law's hut, to see what he could find to eat. There was a large pile of beniseed, and Hare made a most satisfying meal of it while everyone else was busy talking about their new wives. Even Hare was surprised a little later, to see how small the beniseed heap had become, and felt somewhat apprehensive as to what the owner would say when she found out.

Of course, he soon thought of a way to get himself out of trouble, and taking a handful of beniseed he ambled across to where the animals were still busy talking and rubbed some seeds on to Spider, pretending to brush off some dust.

He was only just in time as the next moment a woman came stamping up to the group of animals, shouting angrily:

'Who has been stealing my beniseed? It's always the same. When you folk come up from the earth something always gets stolen. Now, who did it this time?'

Of course, all the animals protested and said they were innocent, which indeed they were. Then the cunning Hare stood up and went towards his mother-in-law, putting on a kind, patient voice and saying:

'There is only one way of finding out who stole your beniseed. Let us search every animal and look for signs of seeds or leaves which are bound to have clung to the fur of the thief.'

The woman agreed and together she and Hare began to search the animals, none of whom objected since they knew they had stolen nothing.

Suddenly Hare gave a cry.

'Oh no!' he exclaimed. 'Not you, Spider! How could you have done such a thing?'

'What are you talking about?' asked Spider, as the other animals crowded round him, and the woman seized him to have a closer look.

'Yes,' she said angrily. 'You have some beniseed clinging to your body. You must be the thief! Don't try to deny it.'

The other animals were angry too, telling Spider what a stupid thing he had done to steal from Hare's mother-in-law, and they would not listen when he swore he had done no such thing.

At last he managed to get away from them all, and calling out in disgust: 'I got you up here, but you can get yourselves down again,' he began his descent to earth, rolling up his web as he went.

Now the animals were in a fix, for their ladder had gone, and it was a very long way down to earth. They shouted to Spider and begged him to come back and spin another web for them, but he would not answer and at last they lost sight of him among the far-distant trees of the earth.

'Now what shall we do?' they asked one another, for they had no desire to stay in the clouds for the rest of their lives.

'I'm going to jump,' said the monkey, suiting the action to the words, and with a mighty leap he dropped like a stone towards the earth.

'So am I,' exclaimed the antelope, and he gave a bound

after the monkey, and was followed by a number of other animals, all encouraged by Hare.

'That's right! That's splendid!' he kept saying, as animal after animal jumped from the clouds. But he did not tell them that they were jumping to their deaths, and as each one hit the ground he was killed outright.

All except Hare, of course. He stood back and waited beside the elephant, telling that large and cumbersome creature to wait until last in case he fell on one of his smaller brothers. Eventually, when all the animals had gone, Hare told the elephant it was safe for him to jump too.

'I'll come with you,' said Hare, leaping on to the elephant's head and clinging tightly as they sped through the air. The poor elephant landed with such a crash that he was killed at once, but his huge body saved Hare from striking the ground and he was not injured at all.

So the cunning animal ran off into the bush to look for Spider and to try to make friends with him again, simply because he hoped for Spider's help at some other time.

But since that day nobody has ever been able to climb up into the sky, and those who have heard this story have no wish to try.

The Magic Horns

O nce upon a time there lived a boy whose mother had died when he was very young. The other women in the compound gave him food to keep him from starving, but they all expected him to work hard to repay them for what he ate. Consequently the poor boy never had a moment to himself and when night came he was sometimes too tired to sleep.

No sooner had he got back from a long search in the bush for firewood for one woman, than another would shout at him:

'Magoda! Magoda! Go and weed my millet patch and don't you dare come back until it is quite clear,' and off he would have to go.

Some hours later he would return, only to be sent off by another woman to search for her son who had not yet returned from pasture with the goats, and when Magoda finally came back for his supper he often found there was very little left for him and he had to go to bed only half fed.

As he grew older he became tired of being continually ordered about by women, and at last he determined to run away. His only possession was an ox which his father had given him and told him to take great care of, so Magoda planned to leave the village one morning before the sun rose while the villagers were still asleep.

The ox seemed to understand the need for silence when Magoda climbed on to his back in the half light, for it stepped delicately out of the compound without cracking a stick with its hooves or flicking the fence with its tail. So Magoda escaped and took to the road, riding on his ox.

As they went along they passed many villages and Magoda could hear the people calling to one another as they set about the day's tasks. He saw women going to the river to get water, while little boys ran along the road behind their flocks of goats and groups of children passed him with big bundles of dry sticks on their heads.

'Aha!' said Magoda to himself. 'Never again shall I have to do that kind of work; I'm free! Free! Free!'

But as the day got hotter poor Magoda became hungry and thirsty and wondered how he would be able to get food, now that he had run away from home.

Suddenly a herd of cattle came along the road towards him with a large fierce-looking bull in the middle of the cows.

Magoda's ox began to speak, but this did not seem surprising at the time.

'Get off my back,' it said. 'Then I can fight that bull and kill it.'

The boy jumped down, the ox rushed towards the bull, headed it away from the cows and a furious fight began. Soon the bull lay dead and the ox was satisfied.

'There now!' it said to Magoda. 'I have proved my strength!'

Magoda climbed on to the ox's back again and away

they went. By now, the boy was very hungry and as they passed a village where the smoke from the fires rose into the still air, the smell of cooking wafted towards him and Magoda raised his hand in despair.

'What wouldn't I give for some supper!' he exclaimed, striking the right horn of the ox to emphasize his words.

To his amazement food immediately began to stream out of the horn; beans and maize and meat, all well cooked. Magoda seized it hungrily as it came and stuffed his mouth with all kinds of good things, but even so he could not eat the food quickly enough to prevent some of it falling on the ground.

'This is wonderful! This is splendid!' he said in delight, and smote the animal's left horn with his free hand.

The food stopped coming out of the right horn at once and what had not been eaten was drawn into the other horn, where it disappeared.

'That's the way it is then,' said Magoda. 'Thank you, good ox! I see that all I have to do is to smite your right horn when I want food and I shall never go hungry.'

They jogged along a track together until the sun was setting, when they came upon another herd of cattle. With a deep sigh the ox said to the boy:

'I must take leave of you here. I have to fight this herd, too, but they will kill me. When I am dead you must break off my horns and take them with you. They will provide you with food whenever you need it if you speak to them, but they will not work for anyone else.'

'Please don't fight!' begged the boy. 'Don't leave me, for you are the only friend I have.'

But the ox would not listen. It dashed at the herd and began fighting so fiercely that at first the boy thought his ox would be victorious. Alas, after a time it grew weaker and weaker until it dropped dead, when the herd trampled over the body and passed on its way.

Sadly Magoda broke off the horns, hid them inside his meagre wrapping cloth and continued his journey. It was now quite dark and he stood still, listening for sounds of a village. Sure enough, away to the west, he heard plaintive singing and the lowing of cattle tied up for the night, so he hurried toward the sounds.

When he reached the village the people were singing a sad song about hunger and the lack of food in their farms, so he knew he would be welcome, provided his horns still gave food now they were no longer attached to a living animal.

'Greetings to you,' he called as he reached the village, and with a stick warded off the inquisitive dogs who rushed barking towards him.

'Greetings,' replied some of the nearby people. 'If it's food and lodging you want, young lad, there's nothing to eat in this hungry spot.'

Magoda walked into the centre of the village and sat down in one of the houses at the invitation of a householder and while they were all busy talking he took out the horns and hit one of them hard saying:

'Give me food, O horn.'

Sure enough, the food just flowed out of the horn, like a stream in spate. The people in the house were amazed and began eating at once; then, when they saw that the supply of food seemed endless, they called their friends to come and share in their good fortune. Never had the villagers seen so much food and not one of them went to bed that night with an empty, rumbling stomach.

When they were all filled, Magoda struck the other

horn, and the remainder of the food disappeared. Then he, too, lay down and slept soundly, for he had had an exhausting day.

Now the householder who had called Magoda inside and in whose house the horns had displayed their magic power, was a greedy man. He had kept a sharp eye on Magoda and soon discovered that the horns were unusual ones, so he lay down and pretended to sleep, listening all the while for the snores and heavy breathing of the other people in the house. When he was certain they were all sleeping soundly he crept out into the compound and rummaged through the rubbish heaps until he found a couple of ox horns. Then he silently took the magic horns from under Magoda's sleeping-cloth and replaced them with his worthless ones.

The next morning, after bidding the householder and all the villagers goodbye, Magoda took to the bush again. He did not know where he would go except that he wanted to get as far away as possible from the compound where he had been brought up. About mid-day he stopped to rest and, of course, spoke to the horns. But nothing happened.

'I expect I struck the left horn instead of the right,' he said to himself and reversing the horns he struck the other one and said, again:

'Give me food, O horn.'

But still nothing happened and Magoda was puzzled and depressed. Then he noticed that the horns seemed a little smaller than before and decided that the magic ones must have been stolen and replaced by those he was now holding. There was only one thing to do. He would have to go back to the village where he had slept the previous night and seek out the thief.

He waited until it was almost evening and quietly made his way to the edge of the compound, unnoticed by the bustling crowd of villagers. As it grew dark, he crept up to the house where his horns had provided such a magnificent feast and he almost laughed out loud: for inside he could hear the angry, impatient voice of the householder, saying repeatedly:

'Give me food, O horn. Give me food! Do you hear me? Give me food, I say!'

Then Magoda remembered that his ox had told him the horns would provide food only when he himself spoke to them. So he waited his chance.

Presently the householder could be heard throwing the horns down on the ground in disgust; then he came stamping out of the doorway and crossed the compound to speak to some of his relatives who were sitting idly round a fire. Quick as lightning Magoda stole into the house, found his magic horns lying by the wall, replaced them with the worthless ones and ran swiftly away.

That night, after a good feast from the horns, Magoda slept in a tree for protection from the wild animals, and as soon as it was light enough to travel he was on his way again, determined to keep his horns well guarded in future.

Presently he came to a fine-looking village where the people seemed more prosperous than those he had met the day before. Walking boldly into the nearest compound he called loudly to the owner, asking if he would allow him to stay there. The owner, a large, ugly man, shouted at him unkindly:

'Go away! We don't want any beggars here. It's difficult enough to feed our own families let alone worthless, ragged, good-for-nothings like you.'

Magoda glanced down at his tattered clothes and decided that he did look more like a beggar than anything else, so he left the compound and made his way to a quiet spot by the river.

'I wonder if these horns would provide me with other things beside food?' he said to himself. 'Well, I can but try.'

Seizing a horn in one hand he struck it with the other, and said:

'Give me rich clothes, O horn.'

Great was his surprise to see a finely-woven cloth and some beautiful ornaments coming out of the horn. When he put these on he looked like a wealthy man, and decided to go back to the village and try his luck again.

How different was his reception this time! Children stood and stared at him, young men stopped in their tracks to ask him what he wanted and the maidens plying their pestles in their mortars, ceased work and bashfully covered their faces with their hands.

There was one exceptionally beautiful girl, working at the door of her mother's hut, and Magoda made straight for her and asked to speak to her parents. They at once agreed to allow this fine-looking young man to lodge in their home.

Time passed, and Magoda produced food and wealth for all the village and the lovely girl's father gladly gave her to him for a wife. The young couple were able to provide themselves with all they needed by speaking to the horns: a large house, herds of oxen, servants to work in their fields and unlimited food.

So Magoda found happiness at last and he and his wife lived to a grand old age and were blessed with many children.

Snake Magic

A woodcutter and his wife had two children, a boy and a girl, but while the girl was beautiful and kind, the boy was wild and selfish, and refused to obey his parents. They all dwelt together in a pleasant village, and after some years the father managed to make sufficient profit from his woodcutting for them to live very comfortably, so that they were scarcely ever hungry.

Time passed and the father grew old. One day when he came back from his work in the forest, he lay on his bed in the hut refusing all food, and within a few hours the family realized that he was dying.

'Come here, my children,' he called in a quavering voice.

The brother and sister, who had now grown up, approached the bed and knelt beside it while the old man said to his son:

'I am about to die. Which would you rather have when I am gone; my property or my blessing? For both you cannot have.'

Without hesitation the young man replied:

'I will have your property.'

Then the father asked his daughter the same question and she answered:

'I would like your blessing, father.'

So he laid his hands on her head, gave her his blessing and fell back dead upon his pillow.

The family mourned for several days, and after the funeral feast the mother, too, became ill and died within a few hours, so that now the brother and sister were left alone in the world.

A few days afterwards, the brother came into the hut where his sister was sitting and announced:

'Everything that belonged to my father and mother now belongs to me. You must collect it all together and pile it outside the hut and I will take it away to my house on the other side of the village.'

The woman did as she was told, and her brother came with carriers who took away everything—beds, stools, cloths, weapons, water-pots. Nothing was left. As the villagers stood by, watching the hut being emptied, they remonstrated with the brother, exclaiming:

'Surely you will leave your sister something! How can she live in a completely empty hut?'

Some of the people who had known the brother since childhood, began shouting at him and cursing him for his greed, so at last, to quieten them, he gave his sister a cooking-pot, a pestle and a mortar and said grudgingly:

'She asked only for a blessing while I asked for the property. Therefore she is not entitled to any of my parents' goods. But I will give her these three things so that she will not starve, since you pester me so.'

Then he followed the carriers back to his house, leaving

his sister with no food or furniture and heedless of how she would manage to live.

The neighbours were sorry for the girl, but as most of them were also poor they could not help her much. They came to borrow her pestle and mortar and in return they would give her a little corn so that she did not starve, although she was often very hungry. She even searched the floor and rafters of her hut to see whether her brother had overlooked anything which she could sell, but all she found was a large pumpkin seed. This she decided to plant behind the house, where soon it grew to an enormous size and promised to bear much fruit.

About this time her brother made enquiries and was told that his sister was managing to live on the food the neighbours gave her in return for a loan of the pestle and mortar which he had so reluctantly given her.

'I would not have left her anything at all had I realized she was going to profit by it,' he exclaimed; and when evening came, he walked straight into her hut, seized the pestle and mortar and the cooking-pot and took them away without a word.

The poor young woman was desperate. She tossed and turned all night, wondering how she would manage to live, and then she remembered her pumpkin plant. At the first light of day, she left her hut and went to look at the place where she had planted the seed. She was delighted to find the plant covered in big, green pumpkins.

'How lucky I am!' she exclaimed, and cutting several of the largest she took them to the market and sold them for a good price.

When people ate these pumpkins they were surprised at the sweet flavour and soon returned to ask the woman for more. Every day she picked a large pile of pumpkins to sell and the next morning she always found there were many more ripe and ready for eating.

So for several weeks she made a handsome profit and was able to buy herself a bed, furnish her house comfortably and fill her storeroom with grain for use in the lean, dry season.

But one day her brother's new wife sent their servant to buy one of the pumpkins which were by now well known throughout the land. When the sister realized whose servant she was, she gave her a pumpkin for nothing, since she had no wish to take payment from her brother. Of course the servant was delighted, and soon the news reached the selfish brother that his sister had made so much profit from selling pumpkins that she was now able to give them away.

He was furious, and said to his wife:

'Tomorrow morning I shall go to my sister's compound and pull up her pumpkin plant. Why should she sell them and become rich? She asked for blessings, not wealth, and I am determined to see that this is all she shall have.'

Early the next day, he strode over to his sister's hut and called loudly at the door:

'Sister, show me where your pumpkin plant grows.'

'Why do you want to know that?' she answered. 'It is behind the house, near the well.' Then fearing that her brother meant to harm the plant, as indeed he did, she rushed into the compound and stood beside the trailing creepers, which were covered with green leaves and delicious fruit.

Pulling his knife from his belt, the brother exclaimed:

'I am going to cut this pumpkin plant and pull up its

roots. You've no business to have such a prosperous plant in your compound.'

'You will do no such thing,' screamed the woman, seizing the stem of the plant in her right hand. 'If you want to destroy my plant you'll have to cut off my hand too, for I refuse to let go!'

With flashing eyes, the man rushed towards his sister and before she could move aside he had not only severed the plant but had also cut her hand off at the wrist.

She screamed in terror, for she had never believed that even her selfish brother would do such a thing, but he turned away and went home, with never a backward glance.

The neighbours came rushing to her aid, bound up the wrist and tried to comfort her, but the sister, saying she could no longer stay in the village since she feared what her brother might do to her, ran away into the forest.

For several days she slept in trees and lived on wild berries while she wandered about. When at last her arm was healed, she saw a large town in the distance and climbed up a tree to rest in safety and consider what she might do to earn her living, even though she had only one hand. The more she thought about it, the more hopeless her position seemed, and she began to weep miserably, wondering whether it would be better to die than to live.

She heard voices approaching and through the bush came a party of men who had been hunting birds. One of them was a prince, the son of the king who reigned over the town nearby, but of course the girl did not know this.

He flung himself on the ground below the tree and calling to his attendants, he closed his eyes and said:

'Let us rest awhile. Then when we are refreshed we shall be able to hunt with renewed vigour.'

The maiden in the tree above sat as still as a stone, but she could not stop her tears from falling. Presently the prince sat up and opened his eyes, exclaiming:

'It's beginning to rain! How very strange, in the middle of the dry season!'

One of his servants replied:

'There is no rain here, sire!' and the others looked up at the cloudless blue sky to be seen through the leaves and said:

'There are no clouds either. Where can the rain be coming from that is falling upon the prince?'

'Go up the tree and find out!' said the prince to the youngest servant, who promptly began to climb upwards. Soon he came face to face with the weeping woman, and he was so astonished that he could think of nothing to say. So he went down again and stood before the prince, still silent.

'Well?' questioned his master. 'What did you find? Why are you struck dumb?'

At last the servant managed to say:

'O sire! I saw the most beautiful maiden up in the branches. But she was weeping sorrowfully and it must have been her tears which fell upon you.'

At this the prince leapt to his feet and climbed the tree himself, where he found the young woman and was delighted to see that she was indeed beautiful.

'Why are you crying?' the prince asked her kindly.

'My life is so sad,' she replied, 'that I cannot keep from weeping. But the tale would take so long to tell that I fear you would not have time to listen.'

The prince, now more intrigued than ever, was determined to hear the woman's story. So he replied:

'Come down the tree and I will take you to my home. No one shall harm you while I am with you.'

'My brother would harm me if he caught sight of me,' said the woman. 'I had best stay where I am.'

But the prince would not hear of it. Calling to his servant, who carried the prince's finely woven blue and white cloth, he helped the maiden cover herself from head to foot, and then led her towards the city.

Once inside the palace the woman washed and changed her clothes, so that she appeared even more beautiful than before, and the prince was determined to make her his wife. He listened to her story and then told her to have no fear, for she was now in the palace of his own father, the king.

'Now I have found you, I must never lose you,' he said. 'Rest here while I go and tell my father that I am going to marry you.'

When the prince told his parents that he had brought home the woman he wished to marry, they were none too pleased to learn that he had found her weeping in the forest.

'But who is she?' they asked. 'Who were her parents, and how do we know that she is a good woman who will make a suitable wife for you?'

'You have but to look at her beautiful face to know that she is good,' the prince replied, and he led his parents to the room where the maiden was resting.

She rose to her feet and smiled as they approached, and from that moment the king and queen loved her.

So they made a wonderful wedding feast, such as had never been seen in that country before, and all the people were astonished at the bride's beauty. But there was much whispering among the townsfolk, that the prince had married a woman with only one hand, and none knew whence she had come.

Time passed, and the prince and princess lived happily in the palace, and their joy increased when a son was born to them. But the prince was an energetic man and a sincere one, so that when his father asked him to go on a long journey to visit the outlying places in his kingdom, the young man said goodbye to his wife and child, and set off.

Now, all this time, the wicked brother had been wasting his money and selling his property, so that now he was almost a beggar. He decided to travel away from his village to see if he could make some money the easy way, by tricking fools and helpless women. It so happened that he arrived in the town where, unknown to him, his sister lived in the palace, and when he greeted a passer-by with: 'What news, my friend?' the man told him about the prince going on a journey and leaving his beautiful one-handed wife at home in the palace.

'What luck!' thought the brother. 'It must be my sister! Now my future is made.'

After a few days, the brother gained an audience with the king.

'I have come to tell you something which may save your son's life,' he said. 'I understand he found a woman in the forest with only one hand, and has taken her for his wife. What the prince does not know, is that this woman has been driven out of many towns and villages, because she is a witch. She has been married six times before this, and six times has she killed a husband by witchcraft and been hounded out of town. Once, she had her hand cut off as a punishment. Do you want the same thing to happen to your son when he returns from his journey as happened to these other husbands of hers? Kill the woman now, before it is too late.'

'Alas!' sighed the king. 'She is so beautiful and so kind, I cannot believe what you say. And yet—'

'It is true!' shouted the man. 'Have you not heard that witches can make themselves ugly or beautiful, as they wish? I beg you, kill the woman and save your son.'

The king was very worried and could not make up his mind what to do. So he called his wife and together they discussed the matter. The queen believed the wicked brother, for she was far more afraid of witchcraft than her husband and had often felt jealous as she looked at her son's beautiful wife, so that in the end, she persuaded the king to get rid of the princess and her young baby.

'I cannot kill them,' said the king sadly, 'but I will have them driven out of the town.' So he ordered his soldiers to drive them away immediately. Then he rewarded the wicked brother handsomely, and caused two mounds like graves to be made outside the city, so that when his son came home he could say to him:

'Your wife and son are dead. I will show you where they are buried.'

Having done his evil work, the brother spent part of his reward on buying a house near the palace, and with the rest of the money he began to trade again, so that soon he was a wealthy man and well thought of by the king and queen.

But where was the beautiful woman and her baby son? They had been driven into the forest so suddenly that they had nothing with them except a small cooking-pot out of which the mother had been feeding the child when the soldiers carried out their orders. The poor woman had no idea what she had done to be treated in this way, for all the captain in charge of the soldiers would say was: 'The king orders you to leave the palace at once. If you return, you and your child will be killed. Go!' The woman had fled, pursued by shouting soldiers, brandishing sticks, and had run deep into the forest with her child, to collapse exhausted at the foot of a tree as night fell.

All night long she lay there, terrified of the rustlings in the undergrowth and the noisy screech of owls and other birds of prey in the branches above, but when morning came she was surprised to find herself unharmed and her child sitting up, looking eagerly around him.

'What shall I do now?' she asked herself aloud. 'I have neither money nor food and I do not even know which part of the forest I am in.'

Just then her little son pointed a chubby finger towards a movement in the grass, and out came a snake, making straight for the child. The woman opened her mouth to scream but before she could utter a sound, the snake spoke.

'Save me, O woman! Save me!' it cried. 'Hide me in your pot, for I am being chased by an enemy.'

The woman was surprised at hearing the creature speak, but she hurriedly bent down and tipped the pot sideways so that the snake could crawl inside. Then it coiled itself up at the bottom and hissed softly:

'Save me from the sun and I will save you from the rain.'

The woman had no time to ask what it meant, for another snake appeared swiftly out of the long grass. Lifting its head as if to strike, it asked her:

'Have you seen my brother passing by?'

'Yes,' she replied, pointing deeper into the forest. 'He went that way.' So the second snake glided away among the trees and was lost to sight.

'Has he gone?' came a voice from the cooking-pot.

'Yes,' replied the woman, and the snake came out and lay at her feet.

'Fear not. I will harm neither you nor your child,' it said. 'But tell me why you are alone in this forest.'

'I have been driven out of my house, while my husband was not there to protect me,' she replied. 'And I have nowhere to go and nothing to eat.'

'Follow me,' said the snake. 'I will take you to my home and will see that nothing harms you. It is a long journey, but I promised you that I would save you from rain if you saved me from sun, and now I can help you as you helped me.'

The woman knew that she and her son would die if they stayed in the forest alone for long, so she got to her feet, tied the child to her back and followed the snake as it glided this way and that through the forest. Presently they came to a wide lake.

'We must rest here awhile,' said the snake. 'I shall sleep while you and your son bathe and refresh yourselves.'

The water was clear and cool and the woman washed herself and her child, but he was a lively boy and so eager to splash and kick in the water that he slipped from his mother's arms. Having but one good hand she found it impossible to reach him in the deep lake. She screamed; she waded in up to her waist; she felt in the water again and again, but could not find him, and while at first the water had been clear and blue, now it seemed black and cloudy.

'Alas! Alas!' she sobbed as she clambered up the bank towards the place where the snake was sleeping. 'My child has fallen in the lake and I cannot find him. Oh! What shall I do?'

'With which hand did you search for him?' asked the snake.

'With my good one of course,' she said impatiently. 'You know that my brother cut off my right hand. How could I feel for my child with just a stump?'

'Put in your right arm,' said the snake, 'and you will find your child.'

'You are cruel to make fun of me. Have I not suffered enough through the loss of my son without your mocking me because I have only one hand?' she said.

'I am not mocking you,' replied the snake. 'Put in both your arms, I beg you, and you will find your child.'

The woman decided that nothing she could now do would make matters worse, so she walked listlessly to the edge of the lake, stooped down and put in both her arms.

Immediately she felt the child's body floating between her arms, and lifting him out with a cry of joy, she saw that he was completely unharmed. She hugged him to her breast with joy while he laughed and gurgled happily, then suddenly she looked down at her right hand and discovered to her amazement that it was completely healed.

'Joy! Joy!' she shouted. 'I have both my hands again and my son is alive.'

'Now let us go to my home,' said the snake, uncoiling himself and beginning to move away down the path. 'I want all my elders to meet you so that they may thank you for saving my life, by hiding me in your pot.'

'But this reward is more than enough,' said the woman, holding up her right hand for the snake to see. 'I need no thanks from your elders. It was a small thing I did for you, and you have done a great thing for me in return.'

'I promised you that if you saved me from sun, I would save you from rain, and I have not yet fulfilled all my promise,' said the snake.

So the woman followed the snake, for she had nowhere else to go, and by now she knew that the creature would bring her nothing but good luck. On and on they went until at last they came to the Kingdom of Snakes, deep in the heart of the forest where no man had ever been. She was treated with great courtesy, and wonderful food was provided for her and the child every day. Throughout the time she spent there, no snake gave her any cause for fear, while the elders among the snakes thanked her again and again for saving one of their tribe.

At last, the woman decided that she must take her child back into the world of men again, and she told the snake that she must leave.

'We shall be sorry to see you go,' he said. 'But first come and say goodbye to my mother and father. They will offer you many precious gifts, but do not take them. Ask for my father's ring and my mother's casket and you will never want for anything as long as you live.'

Sure enough, when the woman went to take leave of the snake's parents they brought out splendid gifts of cloth, gold and precious stones, which they piled on the ground before her.

'How can I carry all this away with me?' she asked them. 'Keep these riches for yourself. All I ask for is your ring, O father, and your casket, O mother.'

'How did you know about them? Our son must have told you,' said the two snakes. 'But we will give you whatever you ask, since you saved our son from death.'

Then handing over the ring, the father snake said:

'When you are hungry, ask the ring for food and it will be provided.'

The mother brought out a little carved casket and said:

'When you need clothes or a house, tell the casket, open the lid and it will be provided.'

'Thank you! Thank you!' said the woman, carefully hiding the casket among her clothes and putting the ring on her finger. Then picking up her child, she said farewell to all the snakes and left their kingdom for ever. She felt braver now, and with her right hand grown again and the ring and casket in her possession, began her journey towards the town where the prince, her husband, lived, hoping to discover whether he had yet returned from his long journey.

The prince had indeed returned, and great was his sorrow when he rode up to the palace gates on his horse, to be told by his parents that his wife and child were dead. Sadly he went to the place where the mounds of earth had been made to look like graves, and he wept and would not be comforted. For many days he stayed inside his room seeing no one and eating scarcely anything, until his parents began to fear that he would die of grief. But they dared not tell him what had really happened to his wife, neither would those of the palace servants who knew say a word.

'Oh my beautiful wife,' he sobbed. 'And my lovely son! Oh that I had never left you! Then perhaps you would not have died.'

Early one morning the prince stood at his window, trying to cool his fevered body in the fresh morning air. Suddenly he noticed on the horizon a fine house that he had never seen before, and forgetting his grief for a moment, he turned to the servant who had just brought him his breakfast and asked:

'Who built that house? It was not here when I went away and by its size it must belong to a very wealthy man.'

'I cannot tell when it was built,' replied the servant, 'for I only noticed it myself but yesterday. The people in the market told me it belonged to a beautiful woman who lives there with her son and a hundred servants among untold riches.'

'I must visit there today,' said the prince, roused from his sorrow by a sudden, strange desire to see this wonderful house. So the servant went hurriedly back to the king and queen and told them that their son appeared to be recovering from his grief at last and was taking an interest in the beautiful new house they could see from the palace windows.

That evening, as soon as the sun had sunk low enough to make walking comfortable, a large group of people surged out of the palace gates and made their way to the new house. The prince led the way, followed by the king and queen and a host of elders and councillors, all anxious to see this extraordinary thing which seemed to have grown in a night.

It was, of course, the home of the woman who had had her right hand restored in the lake. She had arrived at the boundary of the town two days before, and had demanded from the casket a fine house, beautiful furniture, servants, and jewels. Then she had spoken to the ring and been provided with the most delicious food, not only for herself and her son, but for all her servants as well.

Now she heard the sound of many voices and the

shuffling of many feet and running quickly to the door she saw her own dear prince, followed by his parents and an excited crowd, coming towards her house. Quickly she asked the ring to provide food for a large feast and soon her tables were covered with delicacies while she went to the door to welcome her guests.

With a cry, the prince ran towards her and embraced her again and again. Then he picked up his young son, who was now a sturdy little boy, and laughed delightedly.

'Why was it that my parents told me you were dead?' he asked.

'Come inside and I will tell you the true story while you eat,' she replied, beckoning to all those who stood near.

The crowd needed no second bidding, although the king and the queen hung back and seemed afraid.

'We thought you were a witch,' they said, and quickly told the prince how the wicked brother had deceived them.

Then it was the turn of the woman to tell the guests all that had happened to her since she and her son had been driven from the palace.

'I am no witch,' she exclaimed. 'The man who told those lies to the king must have been my brother,' and she related how he had driven her from her house and cut off her hand, long ago.

The guests rose from the table as one man.

'Let us kill him!' they shouted. 'He lives in this town, close by the palace. Come! Let us find him and slay him.'

'Oh no!' gasped the woman. 'Spare him his life, I beg you.'

'Then we will drive him out of town,' they said, as they hurried away to her brother's house.

Then the prince, his wife, and his son went back to the palace together and lived there long and happily. She never saw her wicked brother again and the prince commanded that no one in that place should kill any snake, for it was thanks to the snakes that his wife had been restored to him.

Hare and the Corn Bins

In the old days, all the animals used to make farms like men do today. They hoed the ground, planted the seed, harvested the grain and stored it in corn bins which looked like little round huts, only instead of having a door in front they had a circular hole at the top under the thatch.

Once upon a time, Hare and the other animals worked hard on their farms all through the rainy season, and when the corn was harvested they put it all together into a row of beautifully made little corn bins.

'Now where shall we all spend the dry season?' the animals asked each other as they sat round the fire one night, tired with their weeks of farm work.

Hare's eyes glittered cunningly as he answered:

'I am going far away to some of my relations. It is a place called "Sittincawnbin," and I shall go alone.'

The other animals discussed the merits of other places they knew and at last each had decided where he would spend the dry season. Next morning they rounded up their cattle and went away to different places, each hoping that he had chosen somewhere where there would be enough pasture to feed his herds.

'Goodbye! Goodbye!' called Hare. 'When we return we shall have plenty to eat and enough seed left over to plant on our farms next season.'

He pretended to go away too, but as soon as all the other animals were out of sight, Hare came back to the corn bins, climbed inside the first one and began to have a feast. When he could eat no more, he slept, and when he awoke he began on the corn again.

At last, Hare found that the first corn bin was completely empty.

'Well, I shall have to move,' he exclaimed, but first of all he filled the empty bin with gravel. Then he began on the second bin and lived a life of ease and plenty until that was finished, when he filled it with gravel as before.

So the wicked animal continued all through the dry season, eating the corn which really belonged to the other animals, and by the time the first rains began to fall, Hare had emptied every corn bin and refilled them all with gravel.

A few days later the other animals began to return from their dry season grazing grounds until all were assembled except Hare.

'Where can he be?' they asked one another. 'Hare is always the first back in the rains.'

'He went a very long way this time,' said one of them. 'Some place called Sittincawnbin, I think he said.'

'Let's all call loudly and see whether he is on his way,' suggested another.

So all the animals shouted 'Hare! Hare! Where are you?'

Now the cunning hare was not far away, indeed he had not been out of sight of the corn bins all the time the other animals had been gone, but he hid behind a bush and answered in a very faint voice, as from a distance:

'I'm coming.'

'Listen!' said the animals. 'He is far away, but he heard us, and they began shouting again:

'Hare! Hare! Where are you?'

This time Hare's answer sounded a little louder.

'I'm coming,' he said, still hiding close by, and splashing some water over his body so that it looked like perspiration.

So they went on calling Hare while he answered louder each time, and then suddenly dashing out from behind his bush, he arrived in the middle of the group, panting 'Ehhe! Ehhe! Ehhe!' as though he had run for miles.

'Now we are all here,' said one of the animals, 'let us look into the corn bins to see whether the grain has kept well.'

'You look,' puffed Hare. 'I've come too far today to do anything else except lie and rest.'

What shouting and crying arose when the animals looked in the bins, one by one, and discovered that every one was empty of corn but full of gravel.

'Who can have stolen it?' they asked. 'How can we plant crops this season when we have no grain?' they sobbed. 'It must be one of us,' they said, 'because nobody else ever comes here.'

Then they began to quarrel and snap and growl and bite, until at last they lay exhausted on the ground, and night came.

'Let us all go to sleep now,' suggested the jackal, 'and the animal on whom the moon first shines will be the guilty one.'

They all agreed to this, for they knew that the moon sees everything that happens on the earth, so they left it for her to decide.

'Come and lie down beside me, Squirrel,' begged Hare. 'I am so tired with my long journey that I shall get cramp if I do not have somebody close beside me to turn me over from time to time.'

The good-natured squirrel lay close to Hare, and very soon all the animals were fast asleep, worn out after their long journey.

All except Hare, of course. He was not at all tired, for he had scarcely moved from the spot for several months, so he was able to keep his eyes open for the moon since he had an uncomfortable feeling that she was going to shine on him.

The night was cloudy and the moon was slow in rising, but suddenly her beams shot out like an arrow, and landed on Hare. They landed on Squirrel too, since the two animals were so close together, and very carefully, so as not to wake Squirrel, Hare rolled quietly a few feet away.

Then he began to sing, softly at first, but getting louder and louder so that several of the animals woke up. Then Hare, rubbing his eyes and pretending to have only just wakened, pointed to where Squirrel slept, with the moon shining full on him.

'There's the thief!' shouted Hare. 'It was Squirrel who ate all our corn. The moon knows, you can be sure.'

Before poor Squirrel could utter a word in his own defence the animals had leapt upon him and torn him to pieces, so nobody ever knew it was Hare.

But when any of the animals were heard to mutter: 'Sittincawnbin; Sittincawnbin; I wonder where that is?' Hare always crept quietly away and waited until he heard them talking about something else.

What the Squirrel Saw

One very hot day, a small green grass-snake had made a good meal and looked about for a comfortable place to rest. He found some long, soft grass underneath a tree and curling himself up, he went fast asleep.

Now there was a squirrel up in the tree, and presently he noticed the sun shining on the snake's glittering skin, making little flashes and sparkles as the light filtered through the leaves. The squirrel began chattering and muttering as squirrels always do when they see something bright or unusual, and so he attracted the attention of a hunter who was walking along the bush path nearby.

'Hello!' said the hunter to himself. 'I wonder what that squirrel is making such a noise about.'

Cautiously the hunter walked to the foot of the tree, and there he saw the snake curled up with the sunlight shining on his skin.

'So that's all it is!' he exclaimed in disappointed tones. 'A mere grass-snake which is neither harmful nor yet good to eat,' and leaving it alone he went on his way.

After a short time another man came along the path and he too heard the squirrel's chattering.

'I'll just have a look to see what that squirrel is talking about,' he said to himself, and holding his spear at the ready he softly approached the foot of the tree.

As soon as he saw the grass-snake he exclaimed in disgust:

'My wife wouldn't thank me if I brought that home for her supper, neither will I waste my energy on it, since it is harmless.'

Then he turned back to the path and continued his journey.

Now all this time, a spitting-cobra had been hiding nearby in the long grass. He had had a very worrying morning being chased on three separate occasions by hunters who not only feared the spitting-cobra's poisonous venom but also liked the taste of his flesh in their stew-pot. He had managed to escape them for the time being, but had a feeling that it would not be long before another of these humans spied him and tried to kill him.

When he saw how two hunters had looked at the grass-snake and made no attempt to kill him, he decided that it must be a magic place where all snakes would be left unmolested. So he uncurled himself, and lifting his head high, he hissed and spat at the little grass-snake, who soon awoke and fled terrified into the bush.

'Psss!' said the spitting-cobra to himself, as he curled up on the very spot which the grass-make had recently left so hurriedly: 'Now I can have a good sleep, for no one will touch me here.'

The squirrel saw what was happening and continued his chattering even louder than before, but the cobra did not let the noise keep him awake—he was so used to it.

Presently a third man came along the path, disappointed after a day's fruitless hunting.

'What do I hear?' the man asked himself. 'Squirrels don't make that noise unless they have seen something interesting. Perhaps I shall find some supper if I follow his call.'

With silent steps and club poised, the man made his way to the foot of the tree in the branches of which the squirrel still chattered noisily. With a gasp he saw the big spitting-cobra asleep and helpless in the grass, and raising his club aloft he killed it with one mighty blow. Picking it up and stuffing it into his leather hunting-bag, he laughed for joy at the thought of the delicious supper it would make.

'Thank you, little squirrel,' he called. 'I should not have known this snake were here, unless you had told me,' and he hurried home to his wife.

But the squirrel who had seen and heard everything, chattered and laughed even louder, and said to himself:

'Now I realize that what is safe for one creature is not always safe for another. I must take care never to fall into a trap like that.'

Then he leapt away to the branches of a nearby tree, and scampered off to search for his supper.

Hare and the Hyena

One day, a long time ago when there was a famine in a certain part of Africa, Hare met Hyena.

'How thin you are looking,' said Hare.

'You look as though you would not say "No" to a good meal either,' replied Hyena.

The two animals continued on the road together until they came to a farmer, who was grumbling because all his servants had left him.

'We'll work for you if you will feed us,' suggested Hare.

The farmer willingly agreed, and, giving the two animals a pot of beans to cook, showed them the part of his farm where they must weed.

First of all they made a fire, and fetching three large stones, they rested the pot on them to cook their meal while they set to work. When the sun was high in the sky and it was time for the mid-day rest, Hyena told Hare to keep an eye on the cooking-pot while he himself went down to the river to wash.

Hare sat by the pot, stirring it with a stick and longing to begin his meal, while Hyena, as soon as he was out of sight of Hare, stripped off his skin. He looked the most horrible spectacle, and ran back to Hare uttering strange cries. Poor Hare was terrified.

'Help! Help!' he squealed, as he ran for his fife. 'Never have I seen such a terrible creature! It must be a very bad juju.'

Hyena quickly sat down and ate all the food, which was scarcely enough for one in any case, and then he went back to the river, found his skin and put it on again. He strolled slowly up the bank to the place where the cooking-pot stood, and found Hare returning cautiously.

'Oh, Hyena!' gasped Hare. 'Did you see it too?'

'See what?' asked the deceitful animal.

'That terrible demon,' explained Hare.

'I saw nothing. But come, let us eat now,' said Hyena calmly, as he walked towards the cooking-pot and looked inside it.

'Where is it? Where is my food? What has happened to it?' cried Hyena, pretending to be in a fine rage.

Hare looked at the empty pot.

'It was that horrible demon,' he explained. 'It frightened me away so that it could eat our food.'

'Rubbish! You ate it yourself while I was washing at the river,' shouted Hyena, and no amount of protestations by poor Hare had any effect.

'Well,' said Hare. 'I know what I shall do. I shall make a fine bow and arrow and if the creature comes again I shall shoot it.'

The next day the farmer again gave them a pot of beans, but instead of working while it cooked, Hare took a supple branch and began to make himself a bow.

The cunning hyena watched him as he shaped the wood with his knife, and when it was almost finished, he said:

'Give me your bow, Hare. My father taught me a special way of cutting bows to make them better than any others. I'll finish that for you.'

The unsuspecting Hare gave up his bow and knife and Hyena began cutting it in a special way, making it so weak in one place that it was bound to break as soon as it was used.

'There you are! Keep this beside you while I go and wash, in case that creature comes again,' said Hyena, as he bounded off to the river, to remove his skin once more.

Hare, waiting beside the pot of food, was just considering whether he could take a mouthful, so great was his hunger, when once again the most repulsive-looking animal he had ever seen bounded towards him. Seizing his bow, he put an arrow in it and pulled. Snap! It broke in his hands, and as the horrible creature came closer and closer, Hare fled.

So, of course, Hyena had all the food once more, and then went back to the river and put on his skin. He returned to accuse Hare of stealing the beans. Hare denied having even a taste of food, but looking closely at Hyena he thought he saw a little piece of bean stuck in his teeth as he spoke.

'Aha!' said Hare to himself. 'If that's the way it is, I shall be ready for you tomorrow, my friend.'

That night while Hyena was sleeping, Hare made another bow. It was a good strong bow with no weak spots at all, and had three sharp arrows to go with it. Then the hare, feeling ravenous by now, crept to the spot where they cooked their food, hid the bow and arrows in some nearby long grass and, returning to find Hyena still asleep, he lay down close by him.

The next day, everything happened as Hare had expected. The two animals worked hard all the morning while the cooking-pot boiled nearby, and at mid-day Hyena went to the river to wash.

Hare waited, his new bow in his hand. Presently the loathsome-looking creature came towards him. Hare raised his bow and shot. Straight into the creature's heart went the arrow and Hyena fell dead on the ground. Hare bent over the body and was not surprised when he saw it really was Hyena.

'Oh well,' he remarked, as he ate the first good meal he had had for days, 'my mother always told me that greed did not pay, and now I know she was right.'

The Calabash Children

In a village at the foot of a high mountain, there lived a lonely woman. Her husband was dead and she had never had any children, so she looked forward with dread to a comfortless old age.

Day after day she swept the house, fetched water from the river, collected firewood from the forest and cooked her solitary meals. She had a large piece of land near the river where she grew her vegetables and tended her banana trees, spending most of her spare time weeding and hoeing and wishing she had sons and daughters to help her. The other women in the village were often unkind to her and mocked her when she was tired, saying that she must be a very bad woman since the gods had never sent her any children.

Now the people in this part of Africa believed that a powerful Spirit lived on the top of the mountain, and early in the morning and late at night they would look upwards to the snow-capped peak and pray. The lonely woman prayed too, every day asking for someone to help her with her labours, and at last the Spirit answered her prayers.

It happened like this. One morning she planted some

114

gourd seeds on her farm by the river, and from the start the young plants seemed to be particularly healthy and quick to grow. Each morning she was amazed at the growth which had occurred during the night, until at last the flowers on the gourd plants turned into fruit. The woman weeded carefully around each plant, knowing that very soon she would be able to harvest the gourds, dry them, cut them and sell them in the market for bowls and ladles which were used by all the people round about.

As she was hoeing one day, she suddenly saw a stranger standing at the edge of her plot. She was surprised and wondered how he had come, for she had seen and heard no one on the path which led towards her. He was tall and handsome and had the bearing of a chief. He smiled at the woman and said:

'I am a messenger from the Great Spirit of the mountain. He has sent me to tell you that your prayers have been heard. Tend these gourds with all your skill and through them the Spirit will send you good luck.'

Then the man disappeared as suddenly as he had come.

The woman was amazed but deciding that what she had seen and heard was no dream, but had really happened, she worked even harder on her farm, wondering how the gourds would be able to bring her the good luck she had been promised.

A week or so later, the gourds were ready for harvesting and the woman cut the stems carefully and carried the fruit home. She scooped out the pulp from inside each one and then put them on the rafters inside her hut so that they would dry and become firm and strong. Then they would be called calabashes and people could use them for bowls, and for carrying water.

There was one particularly fine gourd, which the woman placed on the ground beside the fire inside her hut, where she did her cooking, hoping it would dry quickly so that she could soon use it herself.

The next morning the woman went early to her farm to weed the ground around her bananas, and while she was away the messenger from the Great Spirit came to her hut and laying his hand on the gourd by the fire, he changed it into a young boy. Then he touched the gourds up in the rafters and they, too, changed into children.

When the messenger had disappeared, the hut became full of childish voices calling:

'Kitete! Kitete, our eldest brother. Help us down!'

So the boy by the fire stood up and helped the other children clamber down from the rafters; but nobody in the village knew what had happened.

The children ran laughing from the hut. Some seized brooms and swept the house, others weeded the ground outside and fed the hens. Two of them filled the large water-pots which stood at the door with water from the river, while several little boys ran into the forest and came back with bundles of firewood. Only Kitete did not work. The Spirit had not made him into a clever child like the others, and he just sat smiling foolishly, by the side of the fire, listening to the talk and laughter of his companions as they worked.

When all was done, the children cried:

'Kitete! Kitete! Help us back to our places in the roof,' and one by one the eldest child lifted them up to the rafters, when they immediately turned back into gourds again, and as soon as Kitete resumed his place by the fire, he too became a gourd.

The woman trudged slowly home, burdened by a large

116

bundle of grass she had cut for re-thatching her roof, but when she saw that all her work had been done she cried out in amazement. She looked in every corner of her hut and compound and finding nobody there, she went to her neighbours.

'Somebody has done all my work for me while I was at the farm,' she said. 'Do you know who it was?'

'We saw lots of children running about in your compound today,' answered the village women. 'We thought they were relations of yours, but we did not speak to them.'

The woman was greatly puzzled and went home to cook her evening meal, wondering what had happened in her absence. Suddenly she remembered the words of the messenger who had spoken to her by the river. He had said that the Great Spirit would send her good luck if she tended the gourd plants well. Could this be the luck he had spoken of, she wondered?

The next day, the same thing happened. The children called to Kitete, who helped them down from the rafters. Then they worked hard for the woman, some of them even repairing the weak spots on her roof with the grass she had brought home the day before.

The neighbours heard the young voices again, and creeping silently to the edge of the compound, they watched the children at work. Presently they saw the children go inside the hut and soon all was quiet and deserted again.

When the woman came home and saw what her helpers had done, she went outside, and gazing up at the mountain, prayed to the Great Spirit and thanked him for his kindness. But she still did not know how it had happened, for there was nothing to show her that it was the gourds which had turned into children.

However, the neighbours were getting more and more curious, and as soon as they saw the woman leave for her farm the next day, they crept up to the door of her hut and peered silently inside.

Suddenly the gourd by the fire changed into a boy, and voices were heard in the rafters calling:

'Kitete! Kitete, our eldest brother. Help us down.'

The peeping women were amazed to see the children clambering down from the roof and only just managed to get outside the compound before the children came laughing from the hut to begin their day's work.

That evening when the woman returned, the villagers were waiting for her and told her all that they had seen, but the foolish woman, instead of accepting the gift of the Great Spirit unquestioningly, decided to spy on the children herself.

She pretended to go to her farm the next morning, but soon turned and crept quietly up to the door of her hut, in time to see everything that went on. As the children burst out of the doorway in an excited group, they stopped short on finding the woman still there gazing at them in amazement.

'So you are the children who have been helping me,' she said. 'Thank you all very much.'

They stood still and said nothing, but presently they began their tasks as usual and only Kitete sat idle. When the work was done and the children asked Kitete to help them up into the rafters again, the woman would not let them go there.

'Oh no!' she exclaimed. 'You are my children now and I do not want you to change into gourds again. I will cook you your supper and then you will all lie down on the floor by the fire, as other women's children do.'

So the woman kept the children as her own and they helped her so much with the work in the farm and the compound that soon she became rich, with fields of vegetables, many banana trees, and flocks of sheep and goats.

Only Kitete did not work. He was a foolish child and spent his days sitting by the fire which he kept burning with the sticks brought into the compound by his brothers and sisters. They grew older and taller, and the woman thanked the Great Spirit each day for sending them to her, but as she grew richer she became more impatient with the witless Kitete and often abused him with her tongue for being so helpless.

One afternoon, while the other children were outside working at their various jobs, the woman came into the hut to begin cooking the evening meal. The shadows contrasted so greatly with the bright sunshine outside that she could not see, at first, where Kitete lay beside the fire. Tripping over his body, she dropped her pot of prepared vegetable stew, smashing it into fragments and spilling all the food.

Angrily she stood up, and wiping the food from her face she exclaimed:

'What a worthless creature you are! How many times have I told you not to lie near the doorway? But what can anyone expect from such a child as you. You're nothing but a worthless calabash anyway!' Then raising her voice even higher, as she heard the other children returning from the farm, she shouted:

'And they're only calabashes too! Why I bother to cook food for them I can't imagine.'

But her shout turned to a scream as she looked down at her feet, for Kitete had changed back into a gourd, and

119

she screamed even louder in another moment, for as each child came into the hut, it dropped on to the ground and became a gourd again.

The woman knew why this had happened.

'Oh, what a fool I am!' she cried, wringing her hands. 'I called the children calabashes and now the spell is broken. The Great Spirit is angry with me and my children are no more.'

It was true. The children never appeared again and the woman lived alone in her hut, getting poorer and poorer until at last she died.

The Blacksmith's Dilemma

There was once a blacksmith called Walukaga, who was very skilled at all kinds of metal-work. Every day a small crowd of people would gather at his smithy and watch him at work making hoes for the farmers, knives and spears for the hunters, or armlets and bracelets to decorate the young men and maidens.

Early one morning, as Walukaga was beginning work, pumping his sheepskin bellows to make a glowing charcoal fire, a messenger from the king's court arrived.

'His Majesty says you are to go and see him immediately. He has a job for you to do,' said the messenger.

Walukaga was delighted and hastily putting on his best white robes he hurried off to the palace, wondering what the king wanted him to do. He passed many of his friends about their early-morning tasks in the dusty roads, and to all of them he shouted happily:

'The king has sent for me! He has some work for me to do. Wish me luck!'

Walukaga reached the palace and was shown into a little room by the gate, where he waited some time until the king was ready to receive him. Then he was taken into

121

the inner courtyard where the king sat on a stool carved from a single piece of tree-trunk.

The blacksmith bowed to the ground, and when he rose the king said:

'I have sent for you, the most skilful blacksmith in the district, because I have a very special task to give you.' He clapped his hands and several servants appeared with their arms full of odd-shaped pieces of iron which they placed at the king's feet.

'You are to take this metal and change it into a man,' said the king. 'Not just a statue, but a living man of iron who can walk and talk and think, and who has blood in his veins.'

Walukaga was flabbergasted. He searched the king's face to see whether perhaps this was a joke, but the king's dark, serious eyes showed that he was in earnest, so Walukaga decided to go home and think it over.

'Yes, Your Majesty,' he replied, bowing low once more, and the interview was over.

The king's servants helped the blacksmith carry the iron to his smithy, and Walukaga followed them slowly, scarcely returning the greetings of his friends in the town, who wondered what was wrong. Later in the day they came to see him and when he told them what the king had commanded, they too fell silent.

Everyone in that country knew that the king had the power of life and death over his subjects and that if anyone failed to carry out an order, he would be put to death, so poor Walukaga began to think his days were numbered. All day and all night he sat with his head in his hands, wondering how to find a solution to his problem. Of course, a number of people made suggestions. Could he not make an iron shell of a man and persuade somebody to get inside it and speak and walk? Should he run away to a far country and begin life afresh where he was not known? Someone even suggested he bribe the palace cook to put poison in the king's food, since Walukaga himself would surely die within a few days unless the king died first.

Poor Walukaga! He became ill and thin, since he could not sleep or eat, and began roaming the bush alone, speaking his thoughts aloud as he tried to think of a plan to save himself from death.

One evening, as he walked through a deserted stretch of bush, he heard weird singing, and going closer to investigate, he discovered a boyhood friend of his who had now, alas, become mad and lived alone in the wild country outside the town.

'Greetings, Walukaga,' called the madman, who had no difficulty in remembering the blacksmith, even though his mind was so often muddled about other things. 'How kind of you to visit me. Come, sit down and share my supper.'

The madman was harmless enough and Walukaga had nothing else to do, so he sat on a rock beside him and together they ate ripe berries and some honey which the madman had collected from the wild bees. Walukaga suddenly realized that this was the first food he had eaten for several days, and felt better for it, so he decided to humour his old friend and told him the story of the king's demand. To his surprise, the madman sat quite still and listened to the end without interrupting.

'Well,' concluded Walukaga, 'that is my story; and if you can tell me what I am to do, you will be a better friend than any other, for they cannot help me.'

Almost immediately the madman had the answer.

'I know what you must do,' he said. 'Go to the king and tell him that you can only make the kind of man he requires if you have special kinds of charcoal and water. Ask him to make all his subjects shave their heads and bring the hair to be burnt into charcoal and when you have a thousand loads of such charcoal, that will be enough. Then say you must have a hundred pots of water made up from the tears of the king's people, since only such water may be used to keep your fire from burning too fiercely.'

When the madman had said this, he laughed uproariously for some minutes, while the blacksmith tried in vain to thank him for such good advice and then hurried off to the king's palace, in spite of the lateness of the hour.

He bowed low before the king and explained what he must have before he could begin work on the iron man. The king was quite agreeable and sent messages to all his subjects the next morning, commanding them to shave their heads for charcoal and to weep into their water-pots.

The people did their best, wondering at this strange request, and not daring to disobey their powerful king, but try as they would, it was impossible to collect more than two pots of tears or even one load of charcoal.

When the results of this proclamation were brought to the king, he sighed.

'Alas! I can see that we shall never be able to collect all the charcoal and water that Walukaga needs. Send for him to come here at once.'

With shaking legs Walukaga approached the king, and as he looked up was relieved to see a smile on his face.

'Walukaga,' he said. 'You have asked something impossible. I see now that my people can never grow enough hair to produce a thousand loads of charcoal, nor weep enough tears to fill a hundred water-pots. I therefore exempt you from your task.'

'Your Majesty,' replied Walukaga. 'I am indeed grateful to you, for you too, asked something impossible of me. I could never have made a living man from iron, try as I would.'

Then all the people laughed when they realized how cleverly Walukaga had got out of his fix, and the king allowed him to go home and continue his work at the smithy. But the blacksmith never forgot that it was his friend's advice which had saved him, and saw that the madman never went hungry or thirsty to the end of his life.

The Magic Drum

Once upon a time there lived a very rich king. He had fifty wives and many children, acres of farm-land and hundreds of slaves to work there. Everyone in his kingdom was happy and contented, for the king was a kind and peaceful man and ruled with justice.

Now the cause of most of the king's wealth was a magic drum. Whenever the king beat this drum large quantities of the most delicious food appeared, spread on tables ready to eat, and in a country where famines came so frequently, this was wealth indeed.

Not only did the king use the drum to feed his wives, his children and his servants, but he also used it to avert wars. Sometimes a neighbouring tribe would declare war on the king, and the warriors would paint themselves with gruesome patterns and arrive at the edge of the king's dominion flourishing their spears and shouting war-cries.

Then the king would meet them, beating his drum, and immediately tables of wonderful food would appear such as the enemy had never tasted before, and throwing down their weapons, the warriors would fall upon the food with cries of delight. When every man had eaten his fill, the army would go back to their homes, thanking the king for his generosity, their quarrel quite forgotten.

Not only did the king feed human beings with the food from his drum, but he often invited the wild animals. In those days men understood the language of the beasts, and elephants, lions, leopards, antelopes, and buffaloes all came together, ate their fill, and returned peaceably to the forest.

Everybody longed for a drum like the king's, and a few people were envious of it, but the king kept it well guarded and would not part with it.

Now there was a secret about the drum that nobody knew except the king. It would always provide food when it was beaten by the owner unless he had walked over a stick lying in his path or had crossed over a fallen tree-trunk in his travels. Then, when the drum was beaten, instead of food, three hundred angry warriors would appear and would beat the assembled company with sticks and whips while the guests cried for mercy. But the king always kept this in mind when he was journeying, and because he seldom walked far and always watched his steps when he did go, the drum never had cause to produce hostile warriors instead of food, so all was well.

One morning, one of the king's wives took her little daughter down to the nearby stream to wash her. It was a bright, sunny day, for the rainy season was almost over, and as the mother and child walked along the red, sandy path which led to the water, they looked up at the graceful palm trees showing green against the blue sky. They reached the river and the child sang with delight as the cool water splashed over her body, and when at last she was clean and refreshed, she stepped on to the grass bank of the river, beside her mother.

All this time, Tortoise happened to be up a palm tree collecting nuts for his meal, and just as the child stepped out of the water, he dropped a palm nut right at her feet.

'Look, mother!' she exclaimed. 'How lucky I am! I was feeling so hungry after my bathe and now a palm nut has dropped for me. May I eat it?'

The woman stooped down and picked it up, looked at it carefully to make sure it was good and then handed it to her little girl, who soon made short work of it.

The wicked tortoise, now recognizing the woman as one of the king's wives, hastily climbed down the tree and said angrily:

'Give me back my nut. What have you done with it?'

'I've eaten it,' said the child, 'and it tasted very nice too. I didn't know it was yours.'

Tortoise pretended to be angry, for he had thought of a plan to benefit himself, so he said to the woman:

'Ha! You stole the food of a poor man and gave it to your daughter. I saw you. You can't deny it. Here was I, a poor tortoise, climbing trees to gather nuts for my starving family. I shall go to the king and tell him that one of his wives has been stealing my food, and then there will be great trouble.'

The woman laughed and told her little daughter not to worry.

'My husband is a rich man and will soon compensate you for your loss,' she said to Tortoise. 'In any case, I didn't know the nut was yours, so how can you accuse me of stealing it?'

'We must go straight to the king now,' said Tortoise. 'I don't think he will look upon this as a light matter. You yourself know how serious a crime it is to steal another person's food, in this country.'

So the woman, the child, and the tortoise made their way back to the king's compound, where he sat under a tree, surrounded by his councillors.

Tortoise bowed low, as best he could in his hard shell, and then said:

'O King, is it not true that to steal food from anyone is the worst crime a man can commit in this land?'

The king agreed that it was indeed a serious crime and so Tortoise told a long story of how the woman had stolen food that he needed for his starving family. At the end of the tale, the king was in a fix, since he had already admitted in front of all his councillors that the theft of food was a serious crime. But he was a just man and a wealthy one, so he said calmly:

'Well, Tortoise, since you think one of my wives has robbed you I will repay you a hundredfold what you have lost. Now tell me, what will you have? I will give you anything you like to name—goats, chickens, slaves; what will you choose?'

Without a moment's hesitation Tortoise answered:

'I'll have your magic drum.'

What could the king do? He was a man of honour and had promised Tortoise anything he chose, so he handed over the drum and went sadly into his house. However, he did not tell Tortoise what would happen if he stepped over a stick on the road, and it comforted him a little when he realized that Tortoise would probably find this out in time.

What rejoicing there was in the tortoise's home that night, when he demonstrated the magic powers of the drum. The little tortoise children had never had such full stomachs, and his wife was delighted that her days of collecting firewood and standing over a cooking-pot were ended. As for Tortoise, he boasted loudly about his cleverness in getting the drum from the king and told his wife he would never have to do another day's work in his life.

For three days the tortoise family did nothing but eat and sleep, and then Tortoise decided to show his wealth and cunning to other people, so that all might see how rich and clever he was. He sent invitations to everyone he knew, both human beings and animals, inviting them to a feast, but since he was known by most people to be very poor, only a few guests turned up and they did not expect much to eat in Tortoise's house.

However, few though they were, Tortoise beat the drum and his guests were soon confronted by the most wonderful dishes which they ate with haste and then departed to tell all their stay-at-home friends what they had missed.

How happy Tortoise was! For the first time in his life he was prosperous and people began to respect him, but he got more and more conceited every day and less and less inclined to work.

And the king? Well, he bided his time and hoped that one day things would put themselves right again.

Now that Tortoise was rich, other wealthy people began to invite him to their homes, and so it came about that as he was walking back from a party one evening, he unknowingly stepped right over a branch that lay on the pathway.

He was too tired and well-fed to beat the drum for supper that night but next morning, with his plump-looking family around him, clamouring for food, he beat the drum to get their breakfast.

What shrieks! What cries! What pandemonium! Three hundred warriors filled the compound and beat the tortoise and his family so severely that, in spite of their hard shells, they were all left exhausted on the ground.

When the warriors had disappeared and Tortoise had recovered slightly, the unpleasant animal said to himself:

'Something has gone wrong with that drum and all the good magic is used up. But why should my family and I be the only ones to suffer? If we are beaten, then other people should be beaten too,' and the unkind creature sent messages to all those who had been invited to a meal before and who had not come. This time, he said, the food would be even better than the last.

Of course, the news of Tortoise's previous party had spread far and wide, and those who had missed such delicious food last time were determined not to be left out now. So crowds of visitors streamed into the compound, their mouths watering as they thought of the feast to come.

With an evil grin, Tortoise, who had sent his wife and family away into the bush for safety, beat the drum as loudly as he could and then flung himself under a bench where he could not be seen.

The three hundred warriors lost no time in appearing, and the poor guests were beaten almost unconscious and had to help each other back to their homes, still hungry, and muttering curses on Tortoise who had invited them to such a party.

After that, Tortoise could not so much as put his nose outside his door without some bruised and angry person threatening revenge on him, and so at last he decided that the only thing to do was to return the drum to the king, for it could never be beaten again as far as the tortoise family was concerned.

That evening, when most of the neighbours were in bed, Tortoise crept out with the drum towards the king's house. The king was expecting this, for he had heard the tale of the great beating, and he realized that Tortoise did not know the secret of the drum.

'I am tired of this thing,' complained Tortoise, 'and I want you to exchange it for something else.'

'Very well,' replied the king, who was only too anxious to get his magic drum back again, since *he* had not stepped over a stick.

'It so happens that I have a magic tree I will exchange for the drum,' he said casually, trying not to let Tortoise know how delighted he really was to see the drum again. 'This tree,' he continued, 'will bear soup and foo-foo once every day, but only once. Should anyone return to gather more on the same day, then the tree will wither away and die.'

The tortoise was delighted, for foo-foo is a delicious creamy food made with mashed yam, and a favourite of all African people. So home he went with his wonderful tree, and hid it in a very secret place in the bush, away from all prying eyes.

The next morning Tortoise was his old, arrogant self again, and told his wife to collect ten calabashes together and follow him. Wondering, she did so, keeping a wary eye open for any warriors who might suddenly appear. But none came, and presently she found herself standing before the magic foo-foo tree, where she could scarcely believe her eyes. Quickly she took handfuls and handfuls of the creamy, white mush and filled the largest of her calabashes. Then into another one she poured the appetizing soup which dripped from the branches.

What a feast the tortoises had that night! But when the children asked Tortoise where he got the food, he would not say, since he remembered what the king had told him about using the tree only once each day.

After a few days, the children complained that their portions were not large enough, but still their father refused to let anyone else fetch the food, except his wife and himself. The eldest son was angry and said to the others:

'Does our father think he can keep a good thing such as this to himself? Bring me some wood ashes and I will soon find out where this food comes from and we can all feast ourselves and our friends.'

One of the younger sons brought him some ashes, which he put inside a small, long-necked calabash. This he then fixed at the bottom of his father's bag, first having made a small hole there.

'Now,' he said to his brothers and sisters, 'as our father walks he will leave a trail of ashes and I can follow at a safe distance.'

The next morning, the eldest son did exactly as he had planned, and great was his surprise when he peered through the long grasses and saw his father collecting soup and foo-foo from the magic tree. Silently he returned home, so that he would not be missed at breakfast time, and with the rest of his family he ate a hearty meal.

Later in the day when he began to feel hungry again, he called his brothers and sisters together, and swearing them to secrecy, he led the way to the magic tree. They could scarcely believe their eyes, and laughed with joy as they feasted greedily on the soup and foo-foo.

'What a selfish old man our father is,' they exclaimed as best they could with their mouths so full of food.

'Fancy keeping this to himself, when we are always so hungry.'

At last even they were satisfied and on shaky legs they staggered home to sleep off the effects of over-eating.

The next morning, Tortoise was up early, as usual, and crept off to his foo-foo tree. When he got there, he gasped in dismay, for the tree was not to be seen. It had shrivelled and died and the bush had grown over the spot, which was now a dense mass of prickly raffia palm.

'Alas! Alas!' wept Tortoise. 'Someone has discovered my tree and gathered food from it. Now the spell is broken and the magic is gone.'

Sad and hungry he returned home, and summoning all his family together, he told them what had happened. The children looked guiltily at each other, so that he guessed who had done the evil thing, but they lied and would not admit it.

'Come with me,' said the tortoise sadly, and he led his family back into the bush and showed them the overgrown raffia palm.

'My dear wife and children,' he said. 'I have done my best to feed you, but now you have spoilt the magic and I can use it no more. From now onwards you will all have to live here in the bush and find your own food. I can do no more for you.'

So the tortoise family made their home under the raffia palm and have lived there ever since as no doubt you have noticed.

Why the Sun and Moon Live
in the Sky

A long time ago the sun and the water both lived
on the earth and were very friendly.

The sun often paid a visit to the house where
the water lived and they would sit talking together for
many hours. But the water never came to the sun's house,
and one day the sun asked his friend:

'Why do you and your relations not come and visit
me? My wife and I would be very pleased to welcome you
into our compound.'

The water laughed. 'I'm sorry not to have visited you
before this,' he said, 'but the fact is that your house is too
small. Were I to come with all my people, I'm afraid we
would drive you and your wife away.'

'We are going to build a new compound soon,' replied
the sun. 'If it is big enough, will you come and visit us
then?'

'It would have to be very large indeed for me to come,'
explained the water, 'as my people and I take up so much
room I'm afraid we might damage your property.'

But the sun seemed so sad that his friend never visited him that the water said he would come when the new compound was ready, provided that it was a really big one.

The sun and his wife the moon set to work, and with the help of their friends, they built a magnificent compound.

'Come and visit us now,' begged the sun. 'For we are sure that our compound is large enough to hold any number of visitors.'

The water was still doubtful, but the sun begged so hard that the water began to come in. Through the door into the compound he flowed, bringing with him hundreds of fish, some water-rats, and even a few water-snakes.

When the water was knee-deep, he asked the sun:

'Do you still want my people and me to come into your compound?'

'Yes,' cried the foolish sun. 'Let them all come.'

So the water continued to flow into the compound and at last the sun and the moon had to climb on to the roof of their hut to keep dry.

'Do you still want my people and me to come into your compound?' asked the water again.

The sun did not like to go back on his word, so he replied:

'Yes. I told you I wanted them all. Let them all come.'

Soon the water reached the very top of the roof and the sun and the moon had to go up into the sky, where they have lived ever since.

The Monkey's Heart

At the edge of the sea there grew a huge tree which spread half its branches over the land and the other half over the water. It was the favourite tree of a little monkey, who would swing and play among its branches all day, stopping only when he was hungry to pick and eat some of the delicious fruit which grew there.

Now in the sea there lived a shark. One day the monkey threw fruit into the water and the shark gobbled it up. It was very tasty and the shark began to swim close to the tree every morning, until he made friends with the monkey and persuaded him to throw fruit down for him every day.

'Thank you, friend Monkey,' the shark would say. 'I get so tired of eating nothing but fish all the time. This fruit is delicious.'

The monkey enjoyed the shark's friendship and he also enjoyed throwing the fruit into the sea, aiming it at different patches of water as a child throws stones at the waves rolling up the beach.

One day the shark looked up at the monkey as he swung among the branches of the huge tree and said:

'You have been very kind to me these last few months, providing me with fruit every day, and I should like to do something for you in return.'

The monkey chewed his fingers and looked down with interest at the shark, but said nothing.

'So I have decided to take you and show you my home,' continued the shark. 'Then you will meet the other members of my tribe and they will be able to thank you for your kindness to me.'

The monkey looked doubtful, and replied after a moment's thought, 'I don't think I want to go, thank you. We land animals are not fond of getting our fur wet and, as you know, I cannot swim. I shall be much happier if I stay in my tree.'

'Come now!' said the shark. 'Who said you would get wet? I shall carry you to my home on my back and not a drop of water will touch you, for I shall swim very carefully without splashing my tail about.'

The monkey was still undecided, but the day was hot and the fruit season was almost over. Thinking it would be cooler on the water and that there might be something good to eat at the end of the journey, the monkey at last agreed to go. He climbed down the tree, leapt on to the shark's back, and they were off.

At first the monkey was more frightened than he had expected to be, since it was not easy to cling to the shark's slippery back, and they seemed to be travelling so swiftly through the deep blue water. But presently he got used to the movement and opened his eyes wide at the sight of the fish and plants he could see below.

'Are you enjoying yourself?' called the shark. 'Don't you find it much cooler here than on dry land?'

'Yes,' replied the monkey, 'but I wish your back wasn't so slippery. How much further have we to go?'

'We're just about half-way,' answered the shark, 'and there is something that I think I ought to tell you.

'The chief of our tribe, the biggest and most powerful shark in the sea, is very ill, and we fear he will die. But our medicine-man has told us that if the chief can be given a monkey's heart to eat, he will recover. Therefore I am taking you to him, but because you have always been kind to me, I thought I would prepare you for what lies ahead.'

The monkey was terrified and bit his lips to stop himself crying out with fear, while he thought of a plan to help him escape. At last he said as calmly as he could:

'But how foolish of you not to have told me this before we left the land. How can I give my heart to the chief when I have not brought it with me?'

'You have not brought it with you?' repeated the shark. 'But what else could you do with it?'

'It's obvious that you don't know much about monkeys, or you would have heard that most of us leave our hearts hanging in the tree where we sleep. We only use them at night time,' replied the monkey. Then he sighed. 'But I don't suppose you'll believe me. You'd better go on swimming until we reach your home and then when you have killed me, how angry your chief will be when he finds I have no heart!'

The shark knew only too well how angry the rest of his tribe would be if what the monkey said was true.

'As I said before,' remarked the monkey. 'If you had only told me that you needed my heart, I would have brought it with me. I would have been only too happy to let your chief eat it, since you are such a great friend of mine.'

So the shark turned in the water, and swam towards the land, saying: 'If I take you back to your tree will you go and get your heart?'

'Of course I will,' replied the monkey. 'Let us make haste, so that we do not keep your chief waiting.'

The shark streaked through the sea like an arrow with the monkey on his back, who scarcely dared to believe his good luck. At last they reached the shore and the monkey leapt on to the land and shot up the tree calling:

'Wait for me! I shan't be long. I know exactly where I put it.'

Then there was silence. The shark floated backwards and forwards in the water below, waiting for the monkey—but not a sound did he hear from the tree above, nor did he see the slightest movement among the leaves. Presently he called:

'Monkey! Monkey! Have you got your heart yet?' But there was no reply.

Thinking that the monkey had left his heart in a tree further inland, the shark waited a little longer. But still everything was silent. At last the shark became angry and impatient and shouted loudly:

'Monkey! Monkey! How much longer are you going to keep me waiting?'

A half-rotten fruit landed with a thud on the shark's nose, and a burst of laughter came from among the branches of the tree.

'What sort of a fool do you think I am?' asked the voice of the monkey. 'Did you really expect me to come back with you to your home to be killed?'

'But you said you would fetch your heart,' complained the shark. 'Can you not find it?'

The monkey laughed louder than ever.

'My heart is in the right place, in the centre of my body,' he shouted. 'What's more, it has been there all the time. Now go away! Our friendship is ended! You may find some other monkey foolish enough to go with you, but,' he added, emphasizing each word by hitting the shark on the nose with a shrivelled fruit, 'you *won't* . . . *get* . . . *me*!'

So the shark swam sadly away. But the monkey laughed and chattered in the tree, calling all his friends together, telling them how he had outwitted the shark and warning them against being persuaded to take a sea voyage, if they wanted to live to a good old age.

The Children who Lived in a Tree-House

There was once a man who had three small children, two boys and a girl, but his wife was dead and there was no one to look after the children. So he decided to find a new home where they would be safe by themselves during the daytime, while he worked in the fields or went hunting for meat.

So off he went into the forest to search for a suitable place and presently came upon a tall baobab tree.

'What a splendid house I could build at the top of this tree!' he exclaimed, gazing at the wide, spreading branches above his head. 'My children would be safe from wild animals and witches up there.'

Taking his axe, he cut a pile of long, sharp wooden pegs from the low branches of nearby trees, and driving these pegs one by one into the thick trunk of the baobab tree, he made himself steps up which to climb. The top of the tree was even better than he had expected, for the thick, spreading branches made a fine level platform on which to build a house.

The man climbed down, and singing cheerfully to himself, he swung his axe again and again, cutting down young trees with which to build the walls and rafters of his house and carrying them one by one up the steps he had made. When he had collected sufficient wood he began to pull down lengths of creeper which he skilfully twisted into stout ropes. Then all was ready and he set to work building a roomy hut, high in the trees, out of sight of man and beast.

Early the next day he cut grass to thatch the roof; then he built a large bed from sticks and over it he spread soft, hairy skins from the deer he had killed. Now his three little children would have somewhere comfortable to sleep.

The house was almost ready now and when the father had taken some stools and cooking-pots up the tree, there was nothing left for him to do except make a strong rope-ladder out of the creepers which grew everywhere in the forest. At last, this too was finished. He climbed up the pegs to his hut, drove a large, wooden stake into the floor, tied the ladder firmly to it and threw it down so that it reached the ground.

'Splendid!' he cried aloud. 'Now I can bring my children to their new home.'

He climbed carefully down the ladder, testing its strength with his weight, and as he went, he knocked out the wedges of wood he had been using as steps, so that nobody could climb up the tree unless the rope-ladder were thrown down to them.

The children were delighted with their new home, when their father had carried them up the ladder one by one. The two older ones stretched out their hands to play with the leaves that waved above their heads and the baby lay kicking and crooning with delight on the skin-bed.

Their father prepared the evening meal, high in the tree-tops, and they all fell contentedly asleep in their new tree-home.

The next morning the father said he must go hunting for buffalo to feed them all, so he called his children around him and said:

'You will be quite safe in our tree-house provided you do as I tell you. When I have climbed down the rope-ladder, you must immediately pull it up again, and never let it down for anyone except me.'

'But the leaves are so thick and the ground is so far below, that we cannot see whether it is you or not,' replied the oldest child.

'I will sing you a little song,' said his father. 'When you hear my voice singing

> *"Kithengee, Kithengee,*
> *Throw me the ladder,*
> *That I may climb up*
> *With meat for your supper,"*

then you will know that it is your father below, and not one of the evil witches who live in the forest.'

So the man climbed down to the ground and the children pulled up the ladder as they had been told, and all day long they played happily among the tree-tops. They watched the birds flying about their nests and feeding their young; they saw little brown monkeys playing and chattering together, and all the time fresh breezes blew through the house and the dark-green leaves above sheltered them from the mid-day sun.

At last the evening came and they heard their father's voice calling to them from below:

> *'Kithengee, Kithengee,*
> *Throw me the ladder,*
> *That I may climb up*
> *With meat for your supper.'*

The eldest child, Kithengee, threw down the ladder and their father brought them buffalo-meat and taught them how to cook it.

So the days passed quietly and happily, and the children grew tall and strong on the food that their father brought them each day.

But in the forest, as their father had already told them, there were many witches, and there was one who had watched the father's return several times, and heard him sing his song. This witch wanted to capture the children and make them work for her, so one morning when the father had gone far into the forest to hunt, the witch went to the bottom of the tree and sang in her cracked voice:

> *'Kithengee, Kithengee,*
> *Throw me the ladder,*
> *That I may climb up*
> *With meat for your supper.'*

The youngest child called to the others:

'Let down the ladder for father. He has come home early today with our food.'

But the two older children knew it was not their father's voice even though it was their father's song, so Kithengee said:

'That is not father. It is one of the witches he has warned us about.'

Then seizing a log of wood he hurled it down below, where it hit the witch on the head and frightened her away.

When their father came home that afternoon the children told him what had happened. He praised the eldest child for his astuteness and warned them all to be more careful than ever before.

The next day the same thing happened again. The witch waited until the father had gone far away, and then, altering her voice as much as she could, she sang:

> *'Kithengee, Kithengee,*
> *Throw me the ladder,*
> *That I may climb up*
> *With meat for your supper.'*

Although the children could not see the witch, they knew that the voice was not their father's, and seizing a large stone, the eldest child threw it down with all his might. There was a loud howl and the children laughed as they heard the witch running swiftly away.

Now the witch was determined to get those children for her slaves, so she went to the powerful forest magician and asked him to give her a spell to change her voice. The magician sat and thought for a long time and at last replied:

'You must go back to the forest and walk eastwards until you come to a column of brown ants, marching westwards. Then you must bend down and lick up the ants, so that they bite your tongue and it swells to a great size.

'Next you must continue eastwards until you find a nest of big black ants, and these you must also allow to bite your tongue until it swells even more.

'Finally, you must go on walking eastwards until you meet some scorpions. After allowing these to bite your tongue you must return home and rest for a month. Then your voice will be just like the voice of those children's father, and you will be able to capture them and keep them as your slaves.'

The witch did as she was told, and for a month she lay very ill at her home. Then at last she felt better and set off at once to the foot of the baobab tree. She waited until the children's father was well away from their home, then she sang in her new voice:

> 'Kithengee, Kithengee,
> Throw me the ladder,
> That I may climb up
> With meat for your supper.'

This time, even the oldest child was convinced that it was his father waiting below, and he tossed the ladder down at once.

The witch began to climb up, but as she was not used to such exertions, she puffed and blew and the ladder twisted and twirled about so that the eldest child called down:

'Father! Why is the ladder swinging about so much and why do you puff and pant?'

'I have killed a very big animal today,' replied the witch, 'and it is almost too heavy for me to manage.'

A moment later the children screamed with fright as they saw the face of the witch at the top of the ladder, and she set foot inside the house. Now they knew they were in her power and although they called: 'Father! Father! Come and save us!' at the tops of their voices, he was too far away to hear them.

Tucking the children under her arm, the wicked witch

climbed down the ladder and hurried to her own house, where she locked them up.

That evening, the father returned to find the rope-ladder swinging in the wind. He guessed at once what had happened, and hastily climbing up, he searched the house and found that all his children had disappeared.

'Alas!' he wept. 'The witch must have caught them at last, and taken them away. But where has she hidden them? I must go to the village magician and find out.' Seizing his bow and arrow and carrying a gift for the magician, he set off at once for the village where the children had been born, and found the man he wanted sitting outside his hut.

'Please help me,' begged the father, giving the magician a beautiful leopard-skin for a present. 'A witch has taken my three children away and I do not know where they are.'

The magician unrolled the leopard-skin and spread it on the ground. Then taking a calabash full of stones and seeds he shook it from side to side, uttering strange words. Suddenly, with a flick of his wrist, he tipped the contents of the calabash on to the leopard-skin and studied the way they had fallen. Then he spoke as in a dream:

'I see a little brown hut at the end of the northern path which branches off the main forest track by the river . . . I see three children working in the fields beside the hut, and a witch standing over them . . . That is all.'

'Thank you! Thank you!' said the man, and since it was quite dark by now he returned alone to his house in the trees, where he dozed fitfully until the first signs of the morning appeared. Then he set off down the forest track.

It was a long journey, but at last he heard voices in the distance and lying flat on the ground, he edged his way towards the sounds. Sure enough, he saw just what the magician had described. His three children were weeding in the field while the witch stood at the doorway of a hut nearby, never taking her eyes away from them.

For a long time the father waited, hidden behind a large bush, until at last his eldest son came close enough to hear his whispers.

'Kithengee! Kithengee!' murmured the man. 'Don't lift your head! Go on weeding as though nothing has happened, but listen to me.'

'My father!' replied the boy softly. 'I hear you.'

'Has the witch made you her slaves?' asked the man. 'Do you have to cook her evening meal?'

'Yes,' said the boy. 'We all have to work hard for her, but I, the eldest, am given the largest share. If I refuse to do it, she threatens to kill me with her spear.'

'I will tell you what to do,' said the father. 'When you go into the hut this evening, wait until the witch is not looking and then strike the point of the spear against a stone until it is blunt. Then sit down and do nothing else. Do not cook the evening meal, and do not fear, for I shall be close by.'

The father slowly wriggled his way backwards until he was some distance from the field, then crouching under a wild plum bush, he waited for the sun to set.

When evening came the three children returned wearily to the witch's hut.

'I am going for a stroll,' she said in her harsh voice. 'Cook the supper while I am away, or there will be trouble when I return.'

The father was watching the hut and when he saw the witch making her way down a path, he quickly dashed inside and hid under the bed, whispering encouragingly to his children and promising to have them home again very soon.

After a while the witch returned.

'Where is the food?' she screamed, when she saw the empty pots and the cold hearth. 'I said I would kill you if you disobeyed me, and so I shall!'

She seized her spear and thrust it at the eldest child, but he had blunted it so thoroughly that it scarcely scratched him.

At the same moment, the father rushed out from beneath the bed, raised his bow and arrow and shot the witch through the heart.

With a fearful cry, she fell to the ground, and realizing that her end had come, she gazed into the father's eyes and said:

'Alas, I am dying. When I am dead, you must cut off my little finger and throw it into the fire. Then everything I have killed will return.'

Before the father could reply, the witch gave a deep sigh and fell back, dead.

The children shouted with joy to be free of the witch, while their father told the eldest to kindle a fire so that they could do as the witch had told them. Sure enough, when he threw the finger into the flames, a stream of cattle, goats, sheep, and even people stepped from the fire.

'Who are these?' asked the youngest child.

'They are the people and animals that the witch has eaten,' replied his father. 'She would have eaten you in the end, too, had I not rescued you.'

The people who were brought to life again were overjoyed, and thanking the man with all their hearts, they began their journey back to their own villages.

As for the animals, the children and their father drove them back to the foot of the baobab tree in the forest, and then climbed joyfully up the ladder into their airy home again.

After a while, as their goats and cattle multiplied, they became rich and wanted for nothing. So they all lived happily together in the forest for many, many years.

Why the Bat Flies at Night

Once upon a time, the bat and the bush-rat were great friends. All day long they would go hunting in the bush together, dodging between the tall grasses and the stunted trees, and finding good things to eat. When evening came, they would take turns to cook the meal and then eat it together.

But in spite of their apparent friendship, the bat did not like the bush-rat; in fact, he hated him.

One evening while they were eating their supper, the bush-rat asked:

'Why is your soup always so much nicer than mine? Will you show me how you make it?'

'I'll show you tomorrow,' replied the bat, his evil plan already forming in his mind.

The next day the bat prepared the soup as usual. It was delicious, for he was certainly a very good cook. Then he hid the pot and found another one exactly like it which he filled with warm water.

A few minutes later the bush-rat appeared and greeted the bat cheerfully.

'Good evening. Are you going to show me how you make your soup?'

'Watch me,' said the wicked bat, 'and I will explain how it is done. You see, I always boil myself in the soup-pot just before the meal is served, and because my flesh is so sweet, it flavours the soup.'

The bush-rat was amazed as the bat brought out the pot of warm water and jumped inside crying:

'See! This is the boiling soup.'

After a few moments the bat climbed out again, and then quickly changed over the cooking-pots while the bush-rat was not looking. Then he served out the soup, which was as tasty as usual, and explained to the bush-rat that if he would only jump into his own cooking-pot of boiling soup the flavour would be much improved.

The bush-rat decided to try it and, since it was his turn to provide the supper the next evening, he sent his wife away from the fire just as the soup was nearly ready, telling her that he was going to finish it himself in the way the bat had taught him.

The bush-rat leapt into the pot and, of course, was soon quite dead. His poor wife found him there when she returned, and went weeping and wailing to the chief telling him that it was all the bat's fault.

The chief was very angry at the way in which the bat had tricked the stupid bush-rat, and immediately gave orders that he should be arrested. But although everyone searched high and low, they could not find him, for he had been flying over the chief's house when the order to capture him had been given, and so had quickly hidden himself in the bush.

The next day, and all the following days, the people searched for the bat to arrest him, but he kept quite still, high up in a hollow tree where nobody could find him. However, he had to hunt for food sometimes, and so flew out of his hiding-place each night. That is why you never see a bat in the day-time.

Tug of War

H are was angry with both the elephant and the hippopotamus, for they lived on the same island as he did and ordered him about in the most officious way. The trouble with living on a small island was that they could hardly help meeting each other, since there was not a great deal of room. So Hare decided to play a trick on the elephant and the hippo which would make them respect him.

First of all he went into the centre of the island, where there were large trees with thick creepers growing up their trunks and over their branches. Hare spent a whole morning twisting some of these creepers into a strong rope; then, laughing softly to himself, he sought out the elephant. He found him on the eastern side of the island squirting water over his back and trumpeting with pleasure.

'Good afternoon, Elephant,' called Hare. 'Which of us would you say is the stronger?'

The elephant laughed loudly and squirted Hare with water, knocking him flat on his back.

'What a question to ask!' he said. 'Of course I am

155

stronger than you. Shall I prove it by trampling you to death?'

'Oh no!' exclaimed Hare. 'But you could prove it by having a tug of war with me.'

The elephant laughed indulgently and said there was no doubt that he would soon win a tug of war.

'Here is the rope,' said Hare. 'Tie it round your leg while I go to the forest in the middle of the island. But do not pull until I give three sharp tugs. Then do your worst!'

Hare left the elephant tying the rope round his front leg, and seizing the other end of the rope he dashed through the forest and came out on the other side of the island where the hippo lived. Sure enough, the hippo was lying at the edge of the water, sunning himself.

'Good afternoon, Hippo,' shouted Hare from a safe distance. 'Which of us would you say is the stronger?'

The hippo opened his huge red mouth and yawned, showing his strong white teeth.

'What a question to ask!' he said. 'Of course I am stronger than you. I could eat you in one mouthful. Shall I try?'

'Oh no!' cried Hare. 'But you could prove it by having a tug of war with me.'

The hippo said it would be a waste of his energy since it was obvious that he could pull Hare into the water in no time at all. But at last Hare persuaded him to tie the end of the rope round his body, and the hippo promised not to begin pulling until Hare gave three tugs on the rope.

Hare scampered off into the forest until he was well hidden from both animals, and then gave three sharp tugs to the middle of the rope.

How the elephant tugged and bellowed, while the hippo groaned and heaved! But as they were so equally matched, neither could move the other far. First of all, the hippo found himself being dragged out of the water a little way up the beach, so he pulled even more frantically until he got back to the water's edge, when it was the elephant's turn to be dragged from the sea. They continued like this for some time, making more noise than had ever been heard on the island before. Hare, who could hear it all, was thoroughly enjoying himself, and the elephant and the hippo would have gone on with their tug of war for days, had not the wicked hare seized a knife and slashed through the middle of the rope.

Immediately tremendous roars of rage reached his ears and two loud splashes told Hare that his trick had been a success. But he kept out of the way of the elephant and the hippo for a long time afterwards, as you can well imagine.

The Discontented Fish

Once upon a time there was a colony of little fishes who lived together in their own small pool, isolated from the rest of the fish in the river. It was a still, grey pool, dotted with stones and clumps of weed, and surrounded by thorn bushes and a few palm trees.

Most of these fish were as happy and as friendly as they could be. But there was one fish, much bigger and stronger than all the others, who kept himself aloof, and who would draw himself up in a haughty manner whenever the others came near him.

'My good fellow,' he would say, opening his eyes as wide as he could, and balancing himself erect on his handsome tail, 'do stop making such a commotion in the water beside me. Can't you see I am having my afternoon siesta? Go away! And take that rabble away with you,' he would add, sweeping one glistening fin towards a shoal of cheerful small fish darting in and out among the shadows.

This sort of thing happened so often that one day one of the older fish said sarcastically:

'I wonder you don't leave this tiny pool and go off to the big river. A fish as large and important as you should surely mix with others of his own size and excellent breeding.'

The big fish thought things over for several days, and puffed himself even bigger with pride when at last he decided to leave his home and search for a better one.

'My friend is quite right,' he said to himself. 'I should be happier if I lived among fish of my own size. How tired I am of these stupid little creatures! With all the rain we've been having lately the time must be near when the big river overflows its banks, and the flood-water will soon be coming up into our pool. When it arrives, I'll go with it and let myself be swept down into the big river, and get away from all this.'

He told his companions what he had in mind. The older fish congratulated him on his enterprise with solemn faces, but the younger ones could not conceal their delight at the thought of being free from the big fish's criticisms, and they swam backwards and forwards, talking about it among themselves.

After a few more days of heavy rain the floods arrived. They covered the little pool, and the big fish rose to the top of the water and allowed himself to be swept downstream to the river. Once between the banks in the depths of the river itself, he noticed how different the water tasted, and how much larger the rocks and the weeds were. Then he sighed with relief and anticipation, thinking of the good life that lay ahead.

He was resting for a few moments beside a large stone when he felt the water swirling behind him. Suddenly four or five fish, much bigger than he, passed over his head. One of them looked down and exclaimed harshly:

'Out of our way, little fish! Don't you know this is *our* hunting ground?'

Then the others turned on him too and drove him away.

The poor fish hid beneath a large clump of weeds, and peered out anxiously from time to time. Presently two large black and white fish came rushing towards him, with fearsome jaws wide open. They would surely have eaten him up had he not managed to wedge himself in a crevice in the bank, just out of their reach.

'Oh dear!' he gasped, when the two monsters had at last tired of waiting about for him. 'I do hope there aren't any more fish like that in this river. How am I to live if I have to spend the whole day in hiding, with no chance to search for food?'

All day long he stayed in his hiding-place, but when night came he slipped out and began swimming freely in the black water, looking for some supper.

Suddenly he felt a sharp nip in his tail, and turning swiftly he saw the bewhiskered face of a large tiger-fish. He was just about to give himself up for lost when a huge dark object passed overhead. It was a canoe, although the fish did not know this, and it disturbed the water so much that he was able to streak away from the tiger-fish and hide in the mud.

'Alas!' he said to himself. 'Why did I come to this terrible place? If only I could get back to my own little pool, I would never grumble again.'

At last he determined to find the point where he had first entered the river, and then make his way back to the pool before the last of the flood-waters receded.

He wriggled slowly along the muddy bottom of the river, until he recognized the spot where he had first arrived. Then with a leap he was out of the river and into the large expanse of flood-water which was surging past him.

How he struggled as he tried to force his way against the swirling water, until at last, when his strength was almost gone, he found himself back in the pool again.

There he lay panting on the bottom, too tired to move, and as he turned his eyes this way and that and saw the old familiar landmarks, he said to himself:

'If I had only known what the river was really like, I would never have left the safety of our pool.'

After that the tiny fish played undisturbed wherever they pleased, and never again did the big fish say he was too grand to live among them, even though sometimes he may have thought so!

And so we see that every man should be contented with what he has.

Hallabau's Jealousy

A long time ago, there lived a man who had two sons. Although he was very fond of the boys, he longed for a daughter, so that when one day his wife had a baby girl, he was filled with joy.

Nothing he could do for the baby was too much trouble. Whenever he went to market he would bring her back sweetmeats or gaily-coloured beads, and sometimes a beautiful cloth or gaudy head-tie, but the boys would be lucky if they even had new gowns for the feast days. Nor would he allow the girl to be sent to the bush with the other children to collect wood and water, although her brothers always had to do their share of the hard work.

Time passed, until the child grew into a beautiful young girl with bright eyes and a smooth brown skin, her arms and legs unblemished by scratches such as were seen on those others of her age-group who had to work in the home, and help their parents in the fields amid thorns and rocks.

Now her two brothers, Hallabau and Shadusa, grew jealous of the way in which their father treated them, in contrast with the way he behaved to their sister. Hallabau, the first-born, often lay awake at night, considering how he might get rid of his sister, and at last he thought of a plan.

One morning, when the girl was about ten years old, the two brothers were told by their father to go to the forest and collect firewood. Hallabau turned to his sister where she sat on a goatskin mat in the shade thrown by the thatched roof of their house, and said gently:

'Come with us to the forest, sister, and help us gather wood. My brother and I will climb the trees and break off the dead branches, and if you will stand below to collect the pieces into bundles, our task will be much lighter. Do not be afraid,' he said with a smile, as he saw his sister hesitating, 'we will look after you. No harm can come to you, if you are with us.'

The girl was flattered because her brothers sought her company, and rising to her feet she followed them out of the compound and into the dark, shady forest.

At first Hallabau and Shadusa climbed tall trees and broke off the dead branches, while their sister piled the sticks together and tied the large bundle with creepers.

'Take this bundle of wood to the edge of the forest, Shadusa,' said Hallabau, 'and then return for another bundle which my sister and I will have ready for you.'

The younger brother did as he was told, and as soon as the sound of his footsteps was silenced by the thick screen made by the forest trees, Hallabau seized his sister and flung her over his shoulder.

'Let me go! Let me go!' she screamed, but he took no notice and began to climb up a tall mahogany tree, which he had previously selected for his wicked purpose. The girl lay still, fearing that she would fall to her death if her brother dropped her, so Hallabau climbed higher and higher until he reached a thick branch, well hidden by leaves.

Pulling a bundle of strong creepers from under his clothing, her cruel brother bound her to the branch of the tree so tightly that she could not move, and when she understood the fate that was in store for her, she fainted dead away with fright.

This suited Hallabau admirably, so he climbed down the tree as speedily as possible and ran along the path that his younger brother had taken, where presently he met him returning for more wood.

'Alas! Alas!' called Hallabau. 'I have lost our sister. Come and help me find her or our father will be angry indeed! She went this way,' said the wicked boy, pointing in the opposite direction from the tree where he had bound his sister.

The two brothers searched for several hours, but of course they did not find her, and at last they decided to go home and break the bad news to their father. He was angry with them and made them search again the next day and the next, but soon his anger turned to grief and he sadly realized that his daughter was lost for ever.

But what of the poor girl? How was she faring, tied to a branch of one of the tallest trees in the forest? After some time she recovered from her faint, and began to call loudly in the hope that other people in the forest might hear her and set her free. But nobody passed by and her throat became dry and sore with heat and thirst.

Towards evening she heard the sound of men's voices, and the gentle footsteps of donkeys hurrying along the track below. Looking down, she saw a caravan of traders each driving several donkeys loaded with large bags of kola nuts. Last of all came the leader of the caravan, riding the strongest of his animals and encouraging the men and beasts to make haste, so that they might reach their night's resting-place before sunset.

Twisting her head uncomfortably, so that they could hear her, the girl sang:

> *'Oh, do you know my brother?*
> *Have you heard of Hallabau?*
> *I wish I had never met him.*
> *Oh somebody save me, please!'*

The men stopped in their tracks, craning their necks upwards to see who could be singing so sweetly.

'It is a magic bird,' said some. 'No, it is an evil spirit,' said others.

Then the girl sang again:

> *'Oh, do you know my brother?*
> *Have you heard of Hallabau?*
> *I wish I had never met him.*
> *Oh somebody save me, please!'*

'It sounds like a young maid,' said the leader of the caravan, and he began to climb up the mahogany tree.

Sure enough, he found the girl, cruelly tied to a big branch, and as he loosened her bands he asked:

'Are you a maiden, or are you a spirit?'

'Oh sir!' exclaimed the girl, 'I am a poor maiden whose jealous brother has tied me up and left me to die,' and she told the leader of the caravan how she came to be in such a plight.

Now he was a rich man and a kind one, who had no children of his own, and when he saw how beautiful the girl was he made haste to help her down from the tree and set her upon his own donkey, saying:

'You must not go back to your father's house, for your brother will only try to kill you again. Come home with me. From now on, you shall be my daughter.'

So the caravan went on its way, and when the man at last reached home his wife cared for the girl and she lived with them as their daughter for many years, growing even more beautiful as time went by. People came from far and wide to gaze on the maiden, and gradually it was forgotten that she did not belong to the trader and his wife and they thought of her as their own daughter.

At last she reached the age for marriage, and her foster father declared that none but the best of men should be her husband.

Now all these years, Hallabau, her elder brother, had been growing strong and handsome, and one day he told his father that he wanted to set out on a journey to find a wife. The fame of the girl who was his sister had reached even the small village where he lived, and Hallabau decided to take gifts and try his luck as a suitor.

His father gave him many fine cloths, a large bag of cowries and a basket of kola nuts to take with him, and the whole village turned out with drums and songs to wish him luck on his quest.

He travelled for several days, asking at different villages how to reach the home of this maiden so famous for her beauty, and one evening as the sun was setting he arrived at the home of the rich trader.

How handsome Hallabau looked as he stood at the entrance to the compound, tall and upright, his brown skin shining in the golden light of the sun, his gifts lying piled at his feet.

When the trader heard why he had come, he talked with Hallabau far into the night and at last satisfied himself that he was a young man worthy to be the husband of his beautiful daughter.

Next morning the girl was brought out of her hut, and Hallabau found himself speechless in the face of such beauty. The girl, too, was attracted by the young man's good looks, but as soon as he found his voice and began to talk, she recognized him for what he was—her elder brother!

She said nothing, but watched him handing over the precious gifts to her foster father and at last, bidding the kindly couple a sad farewell, she set off with Hallabau on the journey back to his home. During this time she spoke scarcely at all, but the young man assumed that she was shy and thought nothing of it.

Her real parents greeted her with open arms and began to make preparations for the wedding, but they did not recognize her as their long-lost daughter, and wondered at her silence.

Now when the girl had left her foster parents, they had given her a golden pestle with which to pound the grain to make millet cakes for her husband after their marriage, and she took this from her bundle and began to use it that very evening. She poured some grain into a mortar, and swinging the golden pestle up and down, she pounded the grain, singing sweetly as she did so:

> *'How can I marry my brother?*
> *How can my father be told?*
> *Will even my mother believe me?*
> *Oh, how can I prove who I am?'*

The people in the compound heard her sweet singing,

and gathered softly around to see the beautiful maiden they had heard so much about, and to listen to her song. Imagine their surprise when they saw her eyes red with weeping, and heard her sing again and again:

> *'How can I marry my brother?*
> *How can my father be told?*
> *Will even my mother believe me?*
> *Oh, how can I prove who I am?'*

Then one old woman who heard the song fetched Hallabau's parents, and hidden behind the mat fence, they listened as she sang.

'Surely she cannot be our long-lost daughter?' said the father.

'From the first, I thought there was something familiar about her face,' replied the mother.

'Well, we can easily prove the matter,' suggested the father. 'Don't you remember that our daughter had a scar in the middle of her back from the time when she rolled into the fire as a baby?'

'Of course!' exclaimed the mother. 'Let us go and ask the maiden about it now.'

So the parents went to where the girl was pounding corn, and said:

'May we see your back? We think there is a scar there that will prove you are our own daughter.'

At this, the girl burst into tears of relief and embraced her parents saying:

'I had forgotten the scar on my back. Come, see for yourselves! I am indeed your long-lost daughter.'

Then followed such rejoicing as had not been seen in the village for a long time. Fires were lit and delicious food was cooked; drummers were summoned and everyone danced for joy.

But the wicked brother Hallabau was so ashamed of what he had done all those long years ago, that taking his bow and arrow he quietly left the compound, disappearing into the night, and was never heard of again.

Goto, King of the Land and the Water

Many years ago there lived a king who had two wives, one named Yawuro and the other Danyawo. But, alas, he had no sons or daughters, and as he grew older and wealthier he began to worry about who would succeed him and what would happen to his many possessions when he died.

He often walked through the streets of the town, gazing enviously at the naked, brown-skinned children playing happily within call of their mothers, and once or twice he even persuaded some parents to allow him to adopt one of their children. Unfortunately, none of these children grew up, as some accident or illness always befell them. One was bitten by a poisonous snake, another lost her life in a smallpox epidemic, while a third, an adventurous child, slipped and fell to his death while climbing a tree.

So it came about that the people in his kingdom politely, but firmly, refused to give him any more children for adoption, and who could blame them?

At long last, when the king had given up all hope of

an heir, his wife Danyawo had a baby boy. He was a beautiful child, and as good as he was handsome. They called him Goto, and the king's heart was no longer filled with sadness when he walked through the town and saw other men's children.

As the child grew older, he proved to be brave and clever, as well as good to look upon, while everybody who knew him loved him. Everybody, that is, except Yawuro, who was broken-hearted that she had no child and was jealous of all the affection that was showered upon the boy Goto.

At first, she kept her feelings to herself, but one day when Goto was about twelve years old, the courtier whose duty it was to keep unwelcome strangers out of the palace, passed by Yawuro as she sat weeping in a quiet corner of the compound.

'Come now!' he exclaimed. 'Why is the wife of a king weeping? Surely you have nothing to be unhappy about, surrounded by wealth and served with good food every day. Now, if I were crying, there would be good reason for it.'

Yawuro dried her eyes and asked the gatekeeper:

'And why should you weep?'

'Because I work all day and far into the night for very little pay. My wife is ill and my children often go hungry, but nobody cares! What wouldn't I give for just a handful of your great wealth!'

Slowly a wicked idea began to creep into Yawuro's mind.

'If I gave you a bag of gold,' she said, 'would you do something to make me very happy?'

The gatekeeper immediately said he would do anything for so much wealth, and Yawuro, drawing him behind a henna bush for privacy, whispered in his ear.

171

'I was weeping because I have no child, and since everyone makes so much of Goto, I cannot bear to see him growing up in the palace any longer. I want you to take him into the bush and kill him. Then I will pay you your reward and I shall be happy again.'

The avaricious gatekeeper at last consented to do this and the next day he contrived to engage Goto in conversation and promised the boy he would take him into the bush to hunt.

'Let us go tomorrow,' said Goto. 'I cannot wait to try my hand at shooting some of those gazelles you promised to show me.'

'Why, certainly. We will go at daybreak. But do not tell anyone else at all,' replied the cunning gatekeeper, 'and then we will return with so much meat that your parents will be surprised and delighted.'

The next morning the two of them set off with their bows and arrows, while the mist lay over all the land and the sun was still low in the sky. The gatekeeper led the boy away from the small villages which were scattered around the town, so that none of the king's subjects should recognize the child. On and on they went, along narrow, sandy tracks with tall, grey-green grass and many trees on each side, in a silence broken only by the occasional cooing of a distant dove, or the angry barking of baboons on a nearby rocky hill.

Several times Goto asked: 'Are we not there yet?'

The watchman replied: 'Just a little further, and then I will show you the place where the gazelles are to be found.'

At last, when the boy was thoroughly lost, they came upon a wide, deep valley.

'Down here!' whispered the man, and led the way further and further into the undergrowth.

'Now, we will rest here a few moments before we start the hunt,' said the gatekeeper, and they lay down side by side in the shade of a large rock.

Presently Goto fell asleep, and the gatekeeper knew that now was his chance to kill the boy. But he found that he could not bring himself to do such a foul thing. Twice he lifted his hunting knife to cut the boy's throat, but twice he let his hand fall to his side again. The fact was, that although he was discontented and greedy, he had children of his own whom he loved, and could not bear to harm Goto, who was just about the same age as his eldest son.

Rising to his feet, he crept quietly away, leaving Goto fast asleep and completely lost.

When the watchman reached the palace again, Yawuro was waiting for him. He was afraid to tell her that he had not killed the boy, so he lied and assured her that Goto was dead and that she would never see him again. Then he concealed his reward in the deep pocket of his gown and went home to his family.

The next day the palace was full of consternation. Where was Goto? Nobody had seen him for a day and a night and his mother, Danyawo, was beside herself with grief.

'I know some evil thing has befallen him,' she repeated again and again. 'Two nights ago I had a dream in which I saw Goto lying dead at the palace gates.'

The king, too, was very anxious and sent all his servants out to look for his son, but although they searched the countryside and asked everyone they saw for news of Goto, they did not find him. A reward of a hundred bags of cowries was offered in return for news of the boy, but nobody claimed it and the king became silent and sat wrapped in grief, while Danyawo wept day and night loudly lamenting the loss of her only son.

Now Goto was certainly lost, but far from dead, and when he woke from his refreshing sleep to find that the watchman had disappeared, he was very puzzled. For some time he called and shouted but at length, receiving no reply, he decided that the watchman must have encountered some wild animal and met his death. There was nothing else to do except give up all ideas of hunting and try to find his way out of the forest, but the more he tried, the deeper the forest became and as night fell the boy broke some branches off a tree, spread them on the ground and lay down to sleep.

As he slept he had a dream which was so vivid that he remembered every word of it when he awoke.

A shadowy figure seemed to stand beside him saying:

'Make your way east, my son. Make your way east, until you come to a river. Then stand on its bank and call in a loud voice: ''Kabel! Kabel!'' Someone will answer you, and if you do as they tell you, all will be well.'

Goto lay on his leafy bed, thinking over the dream as the sun rose, and turning towards the pale pink light of the morning he made his way east. Before long he came to a wide river and standing on the bank he called:

'Kabel! Kabel!'

Almost at once, ripples disturbed the surface of the water and a lovely maiden came out of the river and stood before him.

'Come with me,' she commanded, taking his hand to draw him into the water.

Goto hesitated a moment, but remembering his dream he did as she told him and walked down into the river, still holding her hand.

How still and blue it was under the water. Goto was surprised to feel no discomfort as he passed between rocks and weeds along the path where the maiden led him. She said nothing until they rounded a bend on the river bed and came upon a beautiful city.

'This is the chief city in my father's kingdom,' she said with a smile. 'Come with me to greet him!' And she led him into a wonderful palace built of grey rocks, where the king sat upon his throne surrounded by courtiers.

He appeared delighted to see Goto, and telling his servants to prepare the best room for the boy, he ordered a feast to be made at once. Goto soon felt very happy with these river-folk, and when he had answered the king's questions about how he had reached the river, the king invited him to stay with him as long as he pleased and promised that he would be treated as if he were his own son.

Years passed, and Goto grew to manhood among the people of the river. He was still brave and charming and everyone loved him, so that when it became known that the princess Kabel was to marry Goto, the kingdom was filled with happiness and the betrothal was celebrated with singing and dancing.

The feast that was held at the wedding of the two young people was one that the people remembered for the rest of their lives. Kabel made such a beautiful bride that Goto could not take his eyes away from her, and the king gave them half his kingdom in honour of the occasion.

Goto and Kabel lived in a part of the palace specially set aside for them and were as happy as the day is long. Every evening they walked along the river until they came to the part of the bank where they had first met. Then they would come up out of the water and wander along the grassy edges of the bank, enjoying the cool evening air and admiring the flowering trees which grew close by.

Then one day the king fell ill and all his wise men or courtiers could do for him was of no avail. So he died and was greatly mourned by his people, all of whom loved him well. There was no question as to who should succeed him since Goto had already won the hearts of the river-folk, so the princess Kabel and her husband became king and queen, and ruled wisely and well.

But gradually a change came over Goto. He no longer felt happy and content, and when he and Kabel took their evening walks along the river bank he would sometimes say:

'Beloved, I long to see my own father again before he dies. I so often wonder how he is and whether he still thinks of me sometimes.'

'Do not worry about such things,' Kabel would reply. 'We have each other and our love is so great, surely you do not want to leave me and search for those who may already have forgotten you.'

But Goto could not drive the longing to see his father from his heart, and at last he begged Kabel to let him go, and promised faithfully that he would return within seven days.

'Yes, you must go,' replied his wife. 'I cannot keep you here any longer, for I can see how sad this thing is making you. But as I cannot bear to be parted from you, I will come too, and meet your father.'

Goto was delighted that Kabel understood how he felt, and when he told her he did not know how to reach his father's house, she exclaimed:

'We must take my father's magic horse. He has flown to the ends of the earth on it and we have but to speak the name of your father's kingdom and the horse will take us there.'

So they said goodbye to their courtiers and the people of the river who were waiting outside the palace to bid them farewell. Then they mounted the horse, whispered the name of Goto's father in its ear and were whisked away up, up, out of the river and into the sky. On and on they flew until at last, looking down, Goto gave a joyful cry as he recognized the town where he had been brought up, and saw his father's palace still standing in the open space in the centre.

Down they glided, landing outside the palace gates, and great was Goto's surprise when he knocked loudly to see the servant who had taken him and lost him in the forest, still on duty as watchman. The man did not recognize Goto, of course, but asked in a casual voice what his business was.

'I want to see the king,' said Goto, 'for I bring him good news.'

'Then you may tell me the good news, fellow, and I will take the message to the king,' replied the watchman.

'Oh no! I must see the king myself. Go and tell him that a stranger called Yauta craves an audience with him,' answered Goto, giving a false name since he did not yet want the watchman to know who he was.

'Be off!' shouted the watchman. 'And don't let me catch you near the palace again. Why, you're not fit to speak to the likes of me, let alone the king. Be off, before I thrash you.'

He raised his hand to strike Goto, but Kabel stepped forward and seized the angry man's arm, saying quietly:

'Shame on you! How can you, a servant of the king,

behave so badly to one who wishes to speak to His Majesty. Now, pray go inside and do as we bid you.'

Kabel spoke with such dignity and assurance that the watchman found himself going into the palace to deliver the message, but he had no sooner got beyond the gate and out of sight of the couple waiting there, than a delicious smell of cooking drove all other thoughts from his mind and he went into the kitchen to see if he could pick up something worth eating, for he was still as greedy as ever. After some time, as he ambled back to the gates chewing a piece of sugar-cane, which the kitchen servants had given him, he suddenly remembered why he had come in and called to a palace servant to know whether the king had wakened from his siesta.

'No, he's fast asleep and snoring,' replied the servant disrespectfully, and the watchman went back to Goto and Kabel who were still waiting outside the gates.

'The king is still asleep,' he said ungraciously, 'and nobody dare wake him yet. Of course, were you to offer me a gift, I might be able to get a message to him when he does wake.'

Goto was about to reply angrily to this suggestion, when an aged dog ambled up to the gate, sniffed the air for a moment or two and then, with a bark of delight, rushed past the watchman and began licking Goto's hands in a frenzy of joy.

'That's odd,' muttered the watchman. 'The old dog has never made friends with a stranger before.'

Goto patted the dog and talked to him, for he remembered the animal from the days when it had been a puppy, and as the dog lay down in delight close to Goto's feet, the young man removed a ring from his hand, wrapped it in a piece of cloth and tied it round the dog's neck. Whispering a word in its ear, Goto gave it a pat, and the animal rose to its feet, edged its way back into the palace grounds and disappeared through a doorway.

'Now what was all that about?' asked the watchman crossly. 'There is something odd going on here. What did you say your name was, young man?'

'I said it was Yauta,' replied Goto, 'and I also asked you to take a message to the king. Since you have done nothing about it I have now made my own arrangements, and if you wait just a little longer you will have a great surprise.'

Meanwhile the dog had made its way into the king's bedroom and softly licking the old man's face so that he awoke, the animal lay down by his side. Soon the king noticed the little package tied round the dog's neck, and when his fingers had fumblingly untied it, he cried aloud as he discovered inside it the ring he had given his son when he was a child.

One of his courtiers ran in and was distressed to see the king sitting up on his bed with tears streaming down his face.

'Your Majesty, what is wrong?' he asked.

The king's wife Danyawo came in at that moment and the king handed her the ring saying:

'Have you ever seen this before, my wife?'

'Yes! oh yes!' she cried. 'It belonged to our beloved son, Goto. Oh, who has given it to you? How did it come into your hands?'

The king turned to the courtier and said urgently:

'Tell the captain of the guard to call out all his men. They must search everywhere until they discover who tied this ring round the dog's neck. When they have found him he must be arrested and brought before me.'

Soon all was shouting and turmoil in the palace grounds and when the watchman pointed out Goto and Kabel to the soldiers, they quickly bound them and brought them before the king.

By now the king had come into his Council Chamber and all his councillors were seated around him, when Goto and Kabel were brought in, somewhat roughly, by several huge soldiers. The king did not recognize his son, for Goto had been but twelve years old when he had last seen him.

'What is your name, young man, and what are you doing here?' asked the king.

'My name is Yauta,' replied Goto, 'and I wish to speak to Your Majesty in private.'

The king was surprised, but he liked the look of the handsome young man and the beautiful girl, so he ordered everyone out of the Council Chamber except his wife Danyawo, whom Goto at once recognized as his mother, even though she was now an old woman.

'My lord king,' said Goto, bowing low, as soon as they were alone. 'I am the owner of that ring. I am your son, Goto, to whom you gave it.'

Danyawo ran towards him, crying to the king:

'It is true! He is indeed our beloved son, returned from the dead.'

'Not from the dead,' replied Goto with a smile, 'but from the Kingdom of the River, and I have brought my wife, Kabel, with me.'

The old couple were delighted and embraced their son a hundred times, while he told them all that had happened since he had been led away from the palace by the wicked watchman.

The king ordered a fine feast for his son and his wife

to which all Goto's old friends and playmates were invited. But the watchman and the evil wife Yawuro were banished from the kingdom for ever.

The people were delighted to see Goto back in his rightful place and they loved and respected Kabel for her beauty and wisdom, so that when the old king died a few years later, Goto became king in his stead and ruled with justice and wisdom. But he had not forgotten his other kingdom under the waters, and with the aid of the flying horse, Goto and Kabel continued to reign as king and queen of both land and water, beloved by all and as happy as they deserved to be.

The Singing Drum and the
Mysterious Pumpkin

Early one morning a crowd of little African girls
went down to the sea-shore to play. Generally,
these children had to work very hard, sweeping
and weeding, gathering sticks and fetching water, but
today was a holiday and they decided to collect shells to
make necklaces and bracelets.

They ran up and down the sandy shore, shouting with
joy, and paddling in the foaming edge of the sea. But they
did not go into deeper water because they had been told
there were sharks which would eat them, and worse still,
evil spirits which might drag them under the water and
turn them into slaves.

There were many beautiful shells lying on the sands.
Some were quite big and shone like pearls, but others,
such as cowries, were extremely small. Soon each child
had a pile of the prettiest, ready to take home. One little
girl found an exceptionally beautiful shell, and, fearing
that the others might tread on it by mistake, she put it on
top of a rock for safety.

So it happened that when they gathered all their shells together, ready to go home, the little girl forgot she had put one on the rock, until they had left the beach some way behind.

'Oh! My shell! My beautiful shell!' she cried. 'I have left the best one on a rock. Please come back with me to get it.'

But none of her companions would return with her.

'You've got plenty of other shells,' they said. 'Just one more won't make any difference.'

'But I must have this one. It's the most beautiful of all,' she said.

'Then go back by yourself to get it,' said the oldest girl. 'We are all tired and hungry and want to get back to our homes.'

So the little girl turned round and walked back to the beach alone, singing to herself as she went, to keep up her courage:

> *'I have left my shell,*
> *My beautiful shell,*
> *Which shines like the moon,*
> *On the bare, grey rock.'*

When she reached the rock, she was horrified to find an ogre sitting on it.

'Come closer, little girl, and sing that song to me again,' he said.

With shaking legs and palpitating heart, the little girl took a step towards him and sang her song again.

'You have a very sweet voice,' said the ogre, picking up the shell which the child had left and which lay on the rock beside him.

'Sing the song once more and I will give you your shell.'

The child sang the song yet again and then as the ogre put out his hand to give her the shell, she reached forward and found her arm held firmly.

'Aha!' growled the ogre. 'Now I have you, I shall keep you. You must sing for me whenever I command you.'

Then, still holding the little girl with one hand, he reached behind the rock with the other and brought out a large wooden drum, into which he pushed the child and hurriedly replaced the drum-skin.

'Now, my pretty one,' he said. 'When I beat the drum, you must sing, otherwise I shall have to beat *you*,' and putting the drum under his arm he set off to walk to a nearby village.

When he arrived, he sat down under the straw roof of the village meeting-place and called out:

'Listen, O villagers! I have a wonderful drum. If you bring me some boiled chicken and rice, I will play it for you, so that you can all dance.'

The people brought him food which he ate greedily, but gave none to the little girl. Then he began to play the drum and the child sang from inside.

'What an unusual drum!' said the villagers as they began to dance and enjoy themselves, not realizing that the ogre had imprisoned a little girl, and was making her sing.

At last, when the people could dance no more, the ogre picked up the drum and went on his way to the next village, where he again sat in the meeting-place and shouted to the villagers to bring him some beer.

After he had drunk well, he started to beat his drum again and the people were amazed at the sweet singing that came from inside the drum in time with the rhythm of his beating.

But he had chosen the wrong village for his evil plan. It so happened that the little girl's parents lived there, and as soon as they heard the singing they recognized it as their daughter's voice.

'What shall we do?' they asked each other. 'He is such a big man, and since he is an ogre he may have magic powers to use against us.'

'I have an idea,' said the mother. 'Give the ogre as much beer as he will drink, and when he has drunk too much he will fall asleep and we can rescue our daughter.'

So the father took calabash after calabash of home-brewed beer to the drummer, pretending that he was repaying him for playing so well and flattering him all the while by saying he had never before heard such a wonderful drum.

Gradually the drum-beats faltered until the ogre lay on the ground in a drunken sleep, and most of the villagers went to their huts for the night.

Softly the little girl's father and mother crept up to the ogre and whispering to their daughter that they were going to save her, they quickly unfastened the drum-skin and released the poor, cramped child. Her mother took her back to their home and hid her in her own hut, then the father said he still had work to do, and left them.

First of all he went into the forest and caught two long snakes which he put inside the drum. Next he dug out a nest of biting ants and managed to get most of them shut in the drum, and finally he added a swarm of bees which he collected from the branch of a nearby tree by making them drowsy with wood-smoke.

When morning came, the ogre awoke and would have gone on his way, but some of the villagers begged him to let them hear the wonderful drum once more. So he began to beat it, but no singing voice accompanied him, try as he would. The villagers laughed at him and said his drum was worthless, so he left them indignantly and decided to take the drum to a lonely spot, open it, and beat the little girl for refusing to sing.

Along the path he went, with the drum under his arm, until he came to a small deserted hollow in the forest.

'Now I'll make you sing!' he shouted angrily, as he opened the lid of the drum.

He could not escape! The bees stung him about the head and shoulders, the ants bit him on his feet and legs, while the two poisonous snakes dug their fangs into his hands as they left the drum, before escaping into the long grass.

It was too much even for an ogre to endure, and in a few moments he lay dead on the ground, with the open drum beside him. It was thus that the little girl's father found him the next day, when he went out to hunt.

But this was not the end of the ogre. As the father returned late that night, he was amazed to find that the ogre's body and his drum had disappeared, and in their place, a pumpkin plant was growing. He told the villagers what he had seen and warned them to keep away from such an evil spot in case some harm befell them.

A few months later, some little boys were playing with their bows and arrows when they came to the place where the ogre had died.

'Just look at these huge pumpkins!' said the oldest boy. 'I have never seen any as big as that before.'

'Leave them alone!' said a smaller boy. 'Have you not heard that this is a magic place?'

'Don't be such a coward!' the boy replied. 'I'm going to pick the biggest pumpkin of all and take it home for our supper.'

In spite of the protestations of his friends, the boy snapped the stem of the massive pumpkin, which immediately rolled towards him and knocked him down. The other boys fled screaming in terror, while the oldest one managed to pick himself up and follow them.

As they turned and looked over their shoulders, they saw the huge pumpkin rolling towards them at a tremendous rate, and they screamed all the louder and tried to run even faster.

In their terror they did not notice that they were, in fact, running away from their own village. Presently they came to a river they had never seen before, by the edge of which sat an old man in a canoe.

'Help! Help!' they shouted. 'A magic pumpkin is after us.'

The man turned his boat towards the bank and the boys just managed to scramble into it before the pumpkin caught up with them, and rolled floating into the water.

Quickly the boatman paddled them across to the other side, where they tumbled out pell-mell on to the grass and continued their flight. But the pumpkin was not far behind, even now. They could hear it crashing through the undergrowth, coming closer every minute.

Soon the boys came to a village, where the elders were sitting in council, debating among themselves to the accompaniment of occasional pinches of snuff.

'Help! Help!' screamed the boys. 'A magic pumpkin is after us.'

Now the elders had heard of magic pumpkins before and they knew that evil spirits and ogres often made their homes in them, so they believed the boys' tale at once. Hurrying them into a hut, they hid them behind the partition and were all seated, quietly talking again, when the huge pumpkin rolled into their midst.

'Give me those boys!' shouted the pumpkin, lurching hither and thither and banging itself against the elders' feet. 'I know where you have hidden them. Give them to me! They are my slaves.'

The terrified boys listened anxiously to hear what the head-man would say, and sighed with relief when they heard him give the order to the other elders:

'Out with your swords! Cut the pumpkin to pieces!'

There was a sound of slashing, shouting and groaning and very soon the pumpkin lay on the ground, hacked into a hundred pieces.

'Come out now, boys,' called the elders, 'and fetch us some firewood to burn this evil thing.'

So the boys made a roaring fire in the centre of the village and piece by piece, the pumpkin was burnt.

'Now we must scatter the ashes far and wide,' said the headman, 'so that they can never come together again to worry us.'

With shouts and laughter the boys tossed the ashes up into the wind which scattered them over the whole countryside, and everyone knew that the magic had ended. Then the boys returned to their own village and told their parents how the pumpkin had been destroyed, and the little girls put on their necklaces of shells and danced for joy that the wicked ogre could never harm anyone again.

The Snake Chief

There were once two sisters who lived in a village beside a river. When they were old enough to be married, their father looked around for suitors, but alas, none came, so he decided he must visit other villages and let it be known that he had two daughters ready to be wed.

One day, he took his small canoe and crossed the big river. Then he walked along a path until he came to a village. It appeared to be a happy place and the people greeted him kindly.

'Welcome!' they cried. 'What news have you brought?'

'I have no news of importance,' he replied. 'Have you?'

'Our chief is looking for a wife,' the people replied, 'otherwise nothing we can think of is worth repeating.'

Now the man had found out what he wanted to know, and he told the people that he would send a wife for the chief the next day.

He re-crossed the river and went to his house, smiling contentedly. When his daughters came back from their work in the fields he called them and said:

'At last I have found a man who is worthy to be the husband of one of my daughters. The chief in the village across the water is looking for a wife. Which of you shall I send?'

The elder daughter said quickly: 'I shall go, of course, since I am the elder.'

'Very well,' replied the man. 'I shall call all my friends and bid the drummers lead you to your husband's home.'

'Indeed you will not,' said the girl haughtily. 'When I go to the home of my husband, I shall go alone.'

Now in that part of Africa it was unheard of for a bride to go to her wedding without a host of friends and relations all singing and dancing for joy. So the father was astonished when his daughter said she would go alone, even though he knew she had been proud and headstrong from childhood.

'But, my daughter,' he pleaded, 'no woman ever goes alone to her marriage. It is not the custom.'

'Then I shall start a new custom,' said the girl. 'Unless I go alone, I shall not go at all.'

At last the father, realizing that no amount of persuasion would induce the girl to change her mind, agreed to her going alone, and early the next morning she set out. He took her across the river and pointed out the way, then returned home unhappily.

The girl began her journey without looking back and after a little while she met a mouse on the path. It stood up on its hind-legs, and rubbing its two front paws together, asked politely:

'Would you like me to show you the way to the chief's village?'

The girl scarcely stopped walking and almost trod on the mouse as she replied:

'Get out of my sight! I want no help from you.'

Then she continued on her way while the mouse screeched after her:

'Bad luck to you!'

A little further on the girl met a frog, sitting on a stone at the side of the path.

'Would you like me to show you the way?' he croaked.

'Don't you speak to me!' answered the girl, tipping the frog off the stone with her foot. 'I am going to be a chief's wife and am far too important to have anything to do with a mere frog.'

'Bad luck to you then,' croaked the frog, as he picked himself up from where he had fallen and jumped off into the bush.

Soon after this the girl began to feel tired and she sat down under a tree to rest. In the distance she could hear goats bleating and presently a herd of them passed by, driven by a little boy.

'Greetings, sister,' he said politely. 'Are you going on a long journey?'

'What business is that of yours?' demanded the girl.

'I thought you might be carrying food with you,' replied the boy, 'and I hoped you might give me something to eat for I am so hungry.'

'I have no food,' said the girl, 'and even if I had I should not dream of giving any to you.'

The boy looked disappointed and hurried after his goats, turning back to say over his shoulder:

'Bad luck to you then.'

Presently the girl got to her feet and continued her journey. Suddenly she found herself face to face with a very old woman.

'Greetings, my daughter,' she said to the girl. 'Let me give you some advice.

'You will come to some trees which will laugh at you, but do not laugh back at them.

'You will find a bag of thick, curdled milk, but do not on any account drink it.

'You will meet a man who carries his head under his arm, but you must not drink water if he offers you any.'

'Be quiet, you ugly old thing!' exclaimed the girl, pushing the old woman aside. 'If I want any advice from you, I'll ask for it.'

'You will have bad luck if you don't listen to me,' quavered the old woman, but the girl took no notice and went on her way.

Sure enough she soon came to a clump of trees which began to laugh loudly as she approached them.

'Stop laughing at me,' she commanded, and when they did not, she laughed noisily at them in return as she passed them by.

A little further on, she saw a bag made from a whole goatskin, lying at her feet. On picking it up, she discovered it was full of curdled milk and since this was something she was particularly fond of, she drank it with relish, exclaiming:

'How lucky I found this! I was getting so thirsty with such a long journey.'

Then she threw the bag into the bush and continued on her way. As she walked through a shady grove, she was a little taken aback at the strange sight of a man coming towards her, carrying his head under one arm. The eyes in the head looked at her and the mouth spoke:

'Would you like some water to drink, my daughter?'

192

it said, and the hand that was not carrying the head held out a calabash of water to the girl.

She was not really thirsty but decided to taste the water and see whether it was sweet, so she took a sip, found it delicious and drank the whole calabash full. Then she continued, without a word of thanks to the strange creature.

As she turned the next bend in the path, she saw in the distance the village she was seeking and knew that her journey was almost over. She had to cross a small stream and found a girl bending there, filling her water-pot.

She was about to pass on when the village girl greeted her and asked:

'Where are you going, pray?'

With scarcely a glance at her questioner she replied:

'I am going to that village to marry a chief. You have no right to speak to me, for I am older than you and far more important.'

Now the younger girl was the chief's sister, but she did not boast about this. She merely said:

'Let me give you some advice. Do not enter the village from this side. It is unlucky to do so. Go right round past those tall trees and enter it on the far side.'

The girl took no notice at all but just walked on to the nearest entrance with her head in the air. When she arrived, the women crowded round her to find out who she was and what she wanted.

'I have come to marry your chief,' she explained. 'Get away, and let me rest.'

'How can you be a bride if you come alone?' they asked. 'Where is the bridal procession, and are there no drummers with you?'

The girl did not answer, but she sat down in the shade of a hut to rest her aching legs.

Presently some of the older women came over to her.

'If you are to be the wife of our chief,' they said, 'then you must prepare his supper, as all good wives do.'

The girl realized that this was true, so she asked:

'And from where shall I get the millet to cook my husband's supper?'

They gave her some millet and told her to grind it, showing her where the grinding-stones were, but unlike most women, she only ground the corn for a very short time, so that the flour was coarse and gritty. Then she made some bread, and when the other women saw it, they went away together and laughed at her incompetence.

As the sun set, a mighty wind blew up. The roof of the hut shook and shivered and the girl crouched against the mud walls in fear. But worse was to come. A huge snake with five heads suddenly appeared, and coiling itself up at the door of the hut, told her to bring it the supper she had cooked.

'Did you not know that I am the chief?' asked the snake, as it began to eat the bread. Then it uttered a fearful scream, spat the food from its mouth and hissed:

'This supper is so badly cooked, I refuse to have you for a wife! So I shall slay you!' and with a mighty blow from his tail, he killed her.

When the news of her death at last reached her father, he still had not found a husband for his younger daughter, whose name was Mpunzanyana.

'Let *me* go to this chief,' she begged him. 'I am sure I could please him if I tried.'

Rather reluctantly the father called together all his relations and friends and asked them to make up a bridal

194

procession for his second daughter. They were all delighted and went away to put on their best clothes, while the father summoned the musicians and drummers who were to lead the way.

They set off early in the morning, and crossing the big river, they sang joyfully as they went. They began the long journey along the same little path that the eldest daughter had taken not so long ago, and presently they met a mouse.

'Shall I tell you how to get there?' it asked of Mpunzanyana, as she stopped to avoid treading on it.

'Thank you very much,' she replied, and listened courteously as the tiny animal told them which path to take.

On they went until they came to a deep valley and found a very old woman sitting beside a tree. The ugly old creature rose shakily to her feet to stand before the girl. Then she said:

'When you come to a place where two paths meet, you must take the little one, not the big one as that is unlucky.'

'Thank you for telling me, grannie,' Mpunzanyana answered. 'I will do as you say and take the little path.'

They journeyed on and on, meeting no one for some time, until suddenly a coney stood on the path in front of them all. Stretching up its head, it looked at the girl and said:

'You are nearly there! But let me give you some advice. Soon you will meet a young girl carrying water from the stream. Mind you speak politely to her.

'When you get to the village they will give you millet to grind for the chief's supper. Make sure you do it properly.

'And finally, when you see your husband, do not be afraid. I beg you, have no fear, or at least, do not show it.'

'Thank you for your advice, little coney,' said the girl. 'I will try to remember it all and do as you say.'

Sure enough, as they turned the last bend in the path, they caught sight of the village, and coming up from the stream they overtook a young girl carrying a pot of water on her head. It was the chief's sister, and she asked:

'Where are you bound for?'

'We are going to this village where I hope to be the chief's bride,' answered Mpunzanyana.

'Let me lead you to the chief's hut,' said the younger girl, 'and do not be afraid when you see him.'

Mpunzanyana followed the girl, and the bridal party followed Mpunzanyana, so that all the people came out of their huts to see what the joyful noise was about. They welcomed the visitors politely and gave them food to eat. Then the chief's mother brought millet to Mpunzanyana and said:

'If you are to be the wife of our chief, then you must prepare his supper, as all good wives do.'

So the girl set to work and ground the millet as finely as she could, then made it into light, delicious bread.

As the sun set, a strong wind arose which shook the house and when Mpunzanyana heard the people saying: 'Here comes our chief,' she began to tremble. Then she remembered what she had been told and even when one of the poles which supported the roof fell to the ground, she did not run outside in a panic but stood quietly waiting for her husband to come home.

She almost cried out when she saw the huge snake,

but when it asked her for food, she gave it the bread she had cooked and it ate it with obvious enjoyment.

'This bread is delicious,' said the snake. 'Will you be my wife?'

For one moment, Mpunzanyana was struck dumb, but she smiled bravely when she thought of all the advice she had had, and replied:

'Yes, O chief, I will marry you.'

At her words, the shining snake-skin fell from the chief and he rose up, a tall, handsome man.

'By your brave words, you have broken the spell,' he explained.

That night a feast was begun in the chief's village which lasted for twenty days. Oxen were slaughtered, beer was brewed and all the time the sound of music and drumming made the people's hearts glad.

So Mpunzanyana became the wife of a rich and splendid chief, and in course of time they had many sons, while the village prospered under her husband's wise rule.

The Two Brothers

Early one morning two brothers left their village and went out into the bush to hunt. They each carried a bow and some arrows and wore a big leather bag slung over one shoulder, which they hoped would be full of meat when they returned.

For a long time they trudged along the sandy paths that led away from the village out into the wild bush, and as they walked a snake would sometimes go slithering into the long grass in front of their feet or a bush-fowl would rise suddenly into the air, squawking with fear.

Presently they left the path behind and had to make their way across country full of boulders and thorn bushes, a place where only hunters and travellers penetrated.

Suddenly, they came across a row of red clay cooking-pots standing upside down.

'What's this?' said the younger son. 'Who can have left these pots in a deserted place like this?'

'Do not touch them,' begged the older son. 'I don't like the look of them. There's magic about and we'd best leave them alone.'

But the younger son had always been the braver of the

two and he refused to pass on as his older brother suggested.

'I'm going to look underneath the pots, whatever you say,' he said, and as he bent down to put the pots the right way up, his brother ran a little distance away and stood watching him anxiously.

The boy turned over the first pot and found nothing underneath, and then he did the same to each pot along the line. There seemed no magic about any of them, but as he turned over the last pot he gave a shout of surprise, for out popped a little old woman.

She took no notice of the younger boy, neither did she thank him for letting her out, but turning to the older lad she shouted:

'Don't stand shivering over there like a frightened gazelle. I won't hurt you. Now, follow me and I will show you something worth seeing.'

But the boy was still terrified and would not take even one step towards her.

'Coward!' she exclaimed. Then she turned to the younger boy and commanded him to go with her. He was always ready for an adventure and went at once.

He followed her for some time until suddenly she stopped in front of a big tree. Handing the boy an axe, she said:

'Cut this tree down for me.'

At the first stroke of the axe, a bullock stepped out of the tree-trunk, and each time the boy chopped at the tree a cow, a bullock, a goat or a sheep came out, until at last he was surrounded by flocks and herds.

'These are for you,' said the woman. 'Now drive them all back to your home. I shall stay here.'

The boy was almost too amazed to speak, but he

remembered his manners sufficiently to thank the old woman.

Driving all the animals before him, he soon came back to the place where he had left his elder brother.

'Just look at what the old woman gave me!' exclaimed the boy happily. 'Don't you wish that you had followed her when she called you?'

He told his brother all that had happened, and together they began to drive the flocks and herds back towards their village.

The grass was scorched and brown, for it was the middle of the dry season, and both the boys were very thirsty—while the animals cried loudly from time to time, as they nosed unsuccessfully for food on the parched ground.

A little further on, as they were passing along the edge of a steep precipice, the older boy, peering over the edge, suddenly gave a shout.

'Look! Water!' he exclaimed, pointing down to where the sparkle of a small stream could be seen among the trees and grasses. 'If you tie a rope round me and lower me over the precipice, I can drink my fill.'

The younger brother did as he was asked, and soon the older one came up from the stream again, refreshed and cheerful.

'Now let me down on the rope,' said the younger brother, and slowly the older boy let out the rope so that his brother could quench his thirst too.

Suddenly an evil thought came to the elder boy. He knew that there was no way to climb up from the valley and with a flick of his hand he threw the rope over the edge, turned round, and began driving the animals home, leaving his brother to perish at the foot of the precipice.

The journey home was slow and tiring, but when the older boy arrived and was greeted in surprise by his parents, he lied to them.

'An old woman gave these animals to me,' he said.

'But where is your brother?' they asked.

'Has he not yet returned? He grew tired of our journey and said he would go home again. I have not seen him since mid-day,' replied the boy.

Of course the younger brother did not come back that night, but the parents were not unduly worried as they thought he had changed his mind and gone hunting in another direction after all.

Early the next morning, while the women of the village were getting water at the well, they heard the song of a honey-bird. There were many of these birds in that part of Africa and people had discovered that if they followed a singing honey-bird, it generally led them to a bees' nest where the men could gather honey.

So, hurrying back to their husbands, the women called out:

'Quick! We hear a honey-bird. Follow it and get us some honey.'

Several men, including the father of the boy who was still missing, ran to the place where the bird was singing, and waited for it to begin to fly.

Off it went, followed by the men, who became more and more surprised at the distance the bird was flying. Through the bush they ran, pausing only when the bird rested on a tree for a few moments, then on again through the thick undergrowth until the men scarcely knew where they were.

At last one of them called to the others:

'I've gone far enough. I don't believe this bird is

leading us to honey, and I am getting so weary that I think I'll turn back.'

At this, the bird sang and chirped so much louder than before, and fluttered its wings so violently, that the men were puzzled.

'It almost seems as though the bird wants us to go on,' said the father of the two boys. 'Let us go just a little further.'

So on they went, until at last they came to a precipice and from far down below a faint voice reached them, calling for help. The bird flew up and down excitedly, then swooped into the valley and landed at the feet of the boy.

The father leant over the edge and strained his eyes to see where the bird had gone.

'My son!' he exclaimed. 'I do believe that is my son.'

Quickly the men fashioned a rope from nearby creepers, and very soon they hauled the boy up the precipice, when he told them the whole story of his adventures.

'Alas,' wept the father, 'that I should have a son so wicked as your older brother. You would have died had not the magic honey-bird led us to this place.'

'The other boy must be punished,' said the men angrily. 'It was only his greed that made him leave his brother here, pretending that the cattle were his own.'

But news of the younger son's rescue must have reached home before the men, since the older brother had already disappeared when they returned and he never came back to the village again.

But the younger boy prospered as his flocks and herds increased and his parents wanted for nothing in their old age.

Fereyel and Debbo Engal
the Witch

A long time ago there lived a witch called Debbo Engal. She had ten daughters, who were beautiful girls whom all men sought after, and from time to time youths would make the long journey to the house where they lived, hidden away in the bush. But none of these young men ever returned to their villages again, although nobody knew the reason why.

Debbo Engal knew however. When young men called to see her lovely daughters she would pretend to be delighted to meet them, giving them palm wine to drink and serving them choice food until night fell. Then she would say:

'It is too late and the night is too dark for you to walk back to your homes through the bush. Why not stay the night here and then go home at daybreak in safety?'

The young men would gladly agree, and Debbo Engal would tell them to lie down around the fire she kept burning in the biggest hut in the compound, and soon all would be asleep.

203

The wicked witch would then sharpen her large knife, creep up to the lads and kill them silently one by one with the skill of long practice. Then in the morning she would eat them! Debbo Engal did not feed on rice or corn or yams. Only human flesh satisfied her cruel appetite.

Now in a village some miles away lived a woman who had ten sons, and they heard of the beauty of Debbo Engal's daughters and wanted to visit them. Their mother entreated the boys not to go.

'It is an evil compound. Keep away, my sons,' she begged. 'So many young men have gone, never to return, and I do not want to lose all my sons at once.'

But the lads laughed at her fears and assured her that they could look after each other and that ten men would be a match for any woman. Besides, the daughters were said to be so very beautiful that none of the young men could rest until they had seen the maidens.

Early the next morning the ten brothers set off in high spirits, singing and laughing as they walked along the narrow paths which led through the bush to Debbo Engal's compound.

No sooner had they left their mother, than she gave birth to an eleventh son. But what a strange-looking child he was, being scarcely the size of his mother's little finger. Then he stood upright straight away, and spoke to her.

'Good mother,' he said, his bright little black eyes gazing fixedly at her face, 'where are my brothers?'

'They have gone to Debbo Engal's compound,' she replied in amazement, wondering how it was that he knew he had any brothers.

At this, the little boy gave a shout, exclaiming:

'Then I must go after them to save them,' and he ran swiftly down the path which his brothers had taken.

Very soon he saw the ten lads in the distance and
called after them:

'Hey! Hey! Wait for me.'

The brothers stopped and turned to see who was calling
and when the tiny boy ran up to them, they stared
open-mouthed. Presently one of them managed to say:

'Who are you, and what do you want?'

'My name is Fereyel, and I am your youngest brother,'
he replied.

'Indeed you are not, for there are only ten of us,' they
replied. 'Now go away and leave us in peace.'

'I want to come with you to save you from harm,' said
Fereyel.

At this the brothers were angry and began to beat
him, saying:

'Don't be so silly! How can you be our brother? Now
go away and leave us in peace.'

They beat him so hard that he lay senseless on the
ground, and then the unkind brothers went on their way
towards Debbo Engal's home.

Some time later one of the brothers found a piece of
beautiful cloth lying across the path.

'Look what I've found!' he exclaimed. 'Some careless
person has dropped this fine cloth. This really is a lucky
journey, isn't it?'

He picked up the cloth, slung it over his shoulder, and
continued on his way. But somehow the cloth seemed to
get heavier and heavier and presently he said to the
second brother:

'Will you carry this for me? It is so very heavy on my
shoulder.'

The second brother laughed at him for a weakling, but
very soon he too found the cloth too heavy and passed it

on to the third, and so it went on until it reached the eldest of the ten brothers. When he complained about the weight, a shrill voice from inside the cloth called out:

'I'm inside! That's why you find the cloth so heavy. It is Fereyel, your youngest brother.'

The young men were furious, and shaking Fereyel out of the cloth, they beat him again and again until once more they left him lying senseless beside the path.

'That's the end of him,' they said. 'Lying little scoundrel.'

So they went on their way, for it was a long journey, and they began to hurry since they had wasted some time in beating Fereyel. Suddenly one of the brothers kicked his toe against a piece of metal, and as he bent to pick it up he saw that it was a silver ring.

'What luck!' he exclaimed. 'Somebody has dropped a ring and now it is mine,' and placing it on his finger he swaggered happily along.

But after a few minutes his hand hung heavily at his side and it was all he could do to walk, so weighty had the ring become. Then the same thing happened with the ring as with the cloth, each brother taking turns to wear it but passing it on when it got too heavy until at last it reached the eldest.

'There's something odd about this ring,' he said, and was just taking it off his finger when Fereyel's voice piped up saying:

'I'm inside! That's why it's so heavy,' and he jumped out of the ring on to the ground.

The brothers were about to beat him again when the eldest said:

'He seems determined to follow us and he's certainly

been very cunning about it. Leave him alone and let him follow us to Debbo Engal's place after all.'

So on they went, until at last they reached the compound they were seeking and Debbo Engal came out to greet them.

'Welcome,' she cried, 'welcome to our home! Come and meet my daughters.'

The ten girls were very lovely and the brothers could scarcely take their eyes away from them. They were led away to the largest hut and Debbo Engal brought them delicious food and drink. At first she did not see Fereyel, for he was hidden behind the eldest brother's foot, but suddenly she caught sight of him, picked him up and exclaimed:

'What a charming little fellow you are! Come with me to my hut, and I will see that you are properly looked after. Never have I seen anyone so tiny! You must stay with me and be mine.'

The brothers were surprised when Fereyel allowed himself to be led away without protest, but they soon forgot all about him as they feasted and drank and danced with the ten beautiful girls.

Night came and the brothers talked about going home, but Debbo Engal persuaded them to stay where they were.

'There is no moon,' she said, 'and you might lose your way. There are many snakes and wild animals about at this season, too, so stay with us and return to your home by daylight tomorrow.'

The lads needed little persuasion and soon began another dance, while Debbo Engal brought more palm wine to refresh them. At last, however, the ten boys and girls had to admit that they were too tired to stay awake any longer, and Debbo Engal lent the brothers some mats and pillows on which to rest in the large hut where the girls were already almost asleep.

The wicked witch went back to her hut and gave Fereyel a comfortable mat to sleep on, and a specially soft pillow for his head.

'There you are!' she said. 'Go to sleep now, and do not wake until the morning. I shall sleep on the mat beside you, my little man, so you will be quite safe.'

So saying, she lay down and closed her eyes and soon the compound was wrapped in silence.

Presently Debbo Engal sat up and bent over Fereyel to see if he was asleep. He closed his eyes and kept perfectly still. She stood up and went to the corner where she kept her big knife, but just as she was taking hold of it, Fereyel called out:

'What are you doing?'

Hastily replacing the knife, Debbo Engal said sweetly:

'Aren't you asleep yet, little man? Let me smooth your pillow for you,' and she tidied his bed, shook up the pillow and begged him to sleep in peace.

Once again she lay down beside him, and once again Fereyel pretended to sleep, so that after an hour the wicked witch got up for the second time and took out her knife, ready to sharpen it.

'What are you doing?' called Fereyel again; so making some excuse, Debbo Engal came back to her bed and told him to go to sleep again.

For a long time after that all was quiet, but Fereyel did not sleep. He waited until the steady breathing of the woman on the mat beside him told him that she was asleep, then silently he crept out of the hut, and made his way to where his brothers and the ten beautiful maidens were.

Gently and silently he changed all their clothes, putting the white gowns the boys wore over the girls, and covering his brothers in the blue robes of the women. Then he returned to Debbo Engal's hut, lay down again and waited.

Sure enough, Debbo Engal soon woke with a start, and for the third time she crept to the corner of her hut, seized her knife and began to sharpen it. Fereyel didn't interrupt her this time, and she slipped out of the door, holding the gleaming blade in her hand. Stealthily she entered the young people's hut, bent over the ten sleeping forms wrapped in white clothes and cut their throats with practised skill.

'Ah ha! They'll make me a splendid meal tomorrow,' she muttered to herself as she lay down contentedly and fell asleep again.

As soon as he was sure Debbo Engal would not wake, Fereyel hurried into the big hut and shook each of his brothers by their shoulders.

'Get up! Get up!' he whispered. 'Debbo Engal meant to kill you all, and had I not changed over your clothes she would have done so. Look!' and he pointed to the ten girls who lay with their throats cut. 'The old witch thinks it is you she has killed.'

The brothers needed no second bidding but tumbled hastily out of the door and began their journey home through the bush, anxious to get as far away from Debbo Engal as possible, before she woke up again.

But it was no use. As soon as the witch woke and discovered that Fereyel was no longer by her side, she rushed into her daughters' hut and saw that she had killed them by mistake in the darkness. Uttering a fearful cry, she called up the wind, mounted on its back and flew towards the brothers, who were as yet scarcely half-way home.

Fereyel saw her coming.

'Look out!' he shouted to his brothers. 'Here comes the old witch.'

The brothers were panic-stricken but Fereyel knew what to do. Seizing a hen's egg from under a bush, he dashed it on to the ground between them and Debbo Engal. The egg immediately turned into a wide, deep river and the young men were able to continue on their way.

Debbo Engal was furious and turned about at once and made for home. But the brothers had not got rid of her so easily, for she came back with her magic calabash and began to empty out all the water from the swiftly-flowing river. Soon there was not a drop left and she was able to continue her journey once more.

Fereyel saw her coming and shouted:

'Look out! Here comes the old witch again,' while he seized a large stone and flung it in her path. Immediately it changed into a high mountain and the brothers continued on their journey, certain that Debbo Engal could not get them now.

But the witch was not defeated yet. She went back to her home on another puff of wind and fetched her magic axe. Then she hacked and chopped and chopped and hacked, until at last the whole mountain disappeared and she was able to continue on her way.

But she was too late. Just then Fereyel saw her coming again and gave his brothers a warning shout.

'Look out!' he cried, as they saw their village ahead, and with one final effort they reached their house. Debbo Engal knew she could not touch them there, and went away defeated, muttering fearful curses under her breath.

But Debbo Engal did not let the matter rest there. She was determined to get hold of the young men and kill them, even as she had mistakenly killed her own daughters, so she lay in hiding and waited her chance.

Early next morning the village headman told the brothers to go into the bush and collect logs. Somewhat fearfully, they went, keeping close together and glancing over their shoulders from time to time in case the witch turned up again. They did not see her however, for the very good reason that she had heard the headman's instructions and had immediately turned herself into a log of wood.

As the lads collected the logs they stacked them beside the path.

'Come on,' one of them called to Fereyel. 'Don't be so lazy! Why are you standing still while we do all the work?'

'Because Debbo Engal had turned herself into a log, and I do not want to be the one who picks her up,' he explained.

On hearing this, the brothers threw down the logs they were carrying and raced for home. Debbo Engal, who was furious that she had not yet been picked up, changed herself back into a witch and hid in the bush, still longing for revenge.

A few days later the brothers went off into the bush to collect wild plums. At first they only found trees with somewhat withered fruit, but suddenly they came upon a bush with bright green leaves and luscious, juicy plums hanging from its branches.

'Look at this! What luck!' exclaimed the eldest brother, reaching out his hand to pluck the fruit.

'Stop!' commanded Fereyel. 'Don't you realize that it's

a magic tree, and Debbo Engal is inside it? If you fill your calabashes with the fruit, she'll soon have you under her spell.'

The brothers dropped their calabashes and ran home with haste, and once again Debbo Engal's plans were frustrated.

The next morning when the brothers came out of their compound, they saw a grey donkey grazing on the communal grass at the edge of the village. It seemed to belong to no one and the brothers thought it must have strayed from a nearby village.

'What luck,' said the eldest. 'Let's all have a donkey ride!'

One by one they climbed on to the donkey's back, until all ten of them were perched up there precariously. Then they turned to Fereyel standing beside them and called:

'Room for one more. Jump on!'

'There's no room at all,' replied Fereyel. 'Even I, small as I am, could not get on that donkey's back now.'

Immediately the strangest thing happened. The donkey began to grow longer, and there was plenty of room for Fereyel.

'Ah ha!' he shouted. 'You won't catch me climbing on the back of such an elongated donkey.'

Then much to everyone's surprise, the donkey shrank back to its normal size.

Fereyel laughed. 'You have all been tricked again,' he said. 'Donkeys don't usually understand what human beings are saying. But this one does, so it must be Debbo Engal again. Get off, if you value your lives!'

The brothers tumbled off the donkey's back and the animal went braying back to the bush, where it changed into Debbo Engal.

Now the witch was desperate. She had tried all her magic tricks save one, and she was determined to make this a success.

'If I can only catch Fereyel, I shall be sure of the others,' she said to herself, and sat in deep contemplation planning another wicked scheme.

The next morning a beautiful maiden walked into the village. The villagers crowded round her and asked why she had come.

'I want to see Fereyel,' she replied in a clear bell-like voice. 'Will you lead me to his house?'

Fereyel was amazed to see such an attractive girl, and asked her to come into the visitors' hut. Then he went out and killed a young goat and told his mother to cook the meat for his beautiful guest.

All day long he entertained the maiden, giving her delicious food to eat and talking to her all the while. The villagers, who had never seen such beauty before, came peeping into the hut from time to time and went away exclaiming loudly at the wonderful sight.

When evening came the maiden said she must go back to her home.

'Will you lead me through the bush, Fereyel?' she asked. 'It is too dark for me to go alone.'

Fereyel willingly agreed and the whole village turned out to bid them goodbye. It was very dark and Fereyel led the way along the little winding path that the maiden had told him led to her home. Suddenly she disappeared behind a thick tree-trunk, and was completely hidden. Fereyel stood still, alert and waiting, straining his eyes in the dark.

Then out slithered a horrible, fat python which made straight for Fereyel and would have coiled itself round him and crushed him to death had he not been waiting for this moment.

'Aha! Debbo Engal,' he laughed, and changed himself into a roaring fire. The python had no time to turn round. It could not stop its huge, rippling body from dashing straight into the fire, where it immediately perished.

Great was the joy in Fereyel's village when he went home and told his brothers the tale, and great was the feasting and dancing they had that night to celebrate the death of the wicked witch, Debbo Engal.

BIBLIOGRAPHY

On the Trail of the Bushongo, E. Torday (Seeley Service & Co. Ltd, 1925).

Kilimanjaro and its Peoples, C. Dundas (H. F. and G. Witherby, 1924).

Folk Stories From Southern Nigeria, E. Dayrell (Longmans, Green, 1910).

Hausa Folk Lore, vols. I and II, R. S. Rattray (Oxford, The Clarendon Press, 1913).

Myths and Legends of the Bantu, Alice Werner (Harrap, 1933).

West African Folk Tales, W. H. Barker and C. Sinclair (Harrap, 1917).

Kaffir Folk Lore, G. M. Theal (London, Swan Sonnenschein, 1886).

Nursery Tales of the Zulus, Callaway (Trubner & Co., 1868).

Ikom Folk Stories From Southern Nigeria, E. Dayrell (Royal Anthropological Institute, 1913).

Hausa Sayings and Folk Lore, Fletcher (1912).

Chinyanja Folk Lore Stories and Songs, R. S. Rattray (SPCK, 1907).

The Baganda, Their Customs and Beliefs, Revd. John Roscoe (Macmillan, 1911).

Swahili Tales, Dr Steere (Bell & Daldy, Covent Garden, 1870).

Mongo Proverbs and Fables, E. A. Ruskin (Congo Balola Mission Press, 1921).

Kamba Tales of Supernatural Beings, Gerhard Lindblom (Berlingska Boktrycheriet, 1935).

Other books in the series

Tales from West Africa
Martin Bennett
ISBN 0 19 275076 3

In West Africa stories grow on trees, they say, and in this lively collection of tales you'll meet many cunning tricksters getting into some very sticky situations, including how Monkey managed not to get eaten by Shark, and how Crocodile learnt his lesson.

Tales from the West Indies
Philip Sherlock
ISBN 0 19 275077 1

Inside the pages of this book you'll meet a variety of unforgettable characters, including the wily monkey, unlucky Mr Snake, and, of course, cunning Anansi the spider and his old adversary, Tiger.

This lively collection of tales brings to life the rich tradition of storytelling in the West Indies and Guyana.

Tales from China
Cyril Birch
ISBN 0 19 275078 X

From the Conquerors of Chaos, to fairies, ghosts, demons, and, of course, dragons, these magical tales from China will bring to life all the mystery and wonder of the East.